# THE WARRIORS CLASH

Gabe ran forward, pistol in hand, and saw an Apache lean out from behind a saguaro cactus, aiming a pistol at him. Gabe dived to the ground as the Apache's pistol fired, and the bullet zipped over his head. The Apache ducked behind the cactus, and Gabe shot his own pistol. The bullet drilled through the pulpy cactus plant and into the Apache's stomach. The Apache hollered and fell to the ground.

Gabe ran forward and fired at the Apache again, to make sure he was dead. Then he jumped over the Apache and landed in front of another, this one aiming a rifle at Gabe.

Gabe thought he was a goner. The Apache pulled his trigger. *Click!* It was a misfire. Gabe fired his pistol, and it wasn't a misfire. The Apache was blown back against a cactus plant, and the needles held him suspended in the air . . .

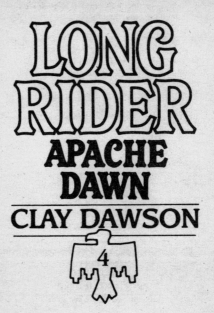

# LONG RIDER

## APACHE DAWN

### CLAY DAWSON

**4**

CHARTER BOOKS, NEW YORK

APACHE DAWN

A Charter Book/published by arrangement with
the author

PRINTING HISTORY
Charter edition/May 1989

ISBN: 1-55773-195-0

Charter Books are published by The Berkley Publishing Group,
200 Madison Avenue, New York, New York 10016.
The name ''Charter'' and the ''C'' logo are trademarks belonging
to Charter Communications, Inc.

PRINTED IN THE UNITED STATES OF AMERICA

10  9  8  7  6  5  4  3  2  1

# APACHE DAWN

# CHAPTER ONE

Gleeson was a scattering of adobe shacks in the middle of the desert. From a distance, it was hard to say whether or not it was inhabited. Gabe Conrad looked down at the little settlement from the hill he'd climbed to get a broad view of the countryside. He'd expected Gleeson to be in the vicinity, and there it was.

He touched the rowels of his spurs to the flanks of his horse, a dun, and the horse descended the hill. It was the month of May and the desert was baking hot. In the distance Gabe could see mountains and buttes through a purple haze. Around him were cottonwood trees, chapparal and cactus plants taller than a man. Birds flitted and chirped as they sipped nectar from the red flowers growing on the arms of the cactus.

A coyote howled in the distance. Its voice echoed across the desert, bouncing off mountains and hills. The sun was a pan of silver gleaming in the pale blue sky. Gabe thought the desert was beautiful, heaven and hell rolled into one. It contained all the colors of the rainbow, and the brightness of the sun and clarity of the air made the colors extremely vivid.

But it was a deadly place. He wouldn't want to run out of water here. He'd been warned about snakes, scorpions and poisonous lizards. It was Apache country, but he hadn't seen any yet.

Gabe had been on the trail seven days, drifting through the southwest, seeing the sights. He had no special place to go and was in no hurry. His map had shown him where the water holes were, and his supplies were ample. Soon he'd be in Gleeson, where he'd buy more goods. It had been a pleasant trip so far.

Gabe was over six feet tall, in his late twenties with gray eyes and long dark blond hair down to his shoulders. He wore a white hat with a wide brim to keep the sun off his face, but his cheeks were deeply tanned anyway. A red bandana was tied around his neck and his shirt was pale blue cotton. A Colt revolver was snug in a holster hanging from a thick brown gunbelt, and a Winchester rifle stuck out of its boot on his saddle. A knife with an eight-inch blade was strapped to his leg where no one could see it.

Gabe rested both his hands on his saddle horn as the dun trudged over the desert. The town was coming closer and Gabe could see people among its buildings. It was a small town with a main street and maybe twenty buildings. It didn't look as though it belonged in the middle of the desert.

Something in the sky caught Gabe's eye. It was a dark object plummeting toward earth. Gabe saw that it was a hawk of some kind, zooming toward prey. A small yellow bird was drinking nectar from a flower on a cactus plant, oblivious to the hawk streaking toward it. Gabe thought he should fire a shot and warn the bird, but decided to let nature run its course.

The yellow bird sensed danger at the last moment. It chirped and tried to get away, but it was too late. The hawk collided with the bird and seized it in its talons. The bird squirmed and tried to get loose, but it didn't have a chance. The hawk flapped its enormous wings and flew away toward purple bluffs in the distance.

Gabe figured the hawk had a nest of little ones in those bluffs. The yellow bird would become food for the baby hawks. Hawks were food for bigger birds. Gabe had been raised by Sioux Indians, and remembered what Little Wound, his stepfather, had said to him once: *You eat life or life eats you.*

The town of Gleeson was drawing closer. Gabe could see people running frantically through the streets. It looked as though a group of men were turning a wagon onto its side in front of a building. Other men herded horses into a corral. Gabe wondered what was going on. He heard someone shouting orders.

He came to the edge of the town and reined back the dun. He saw a group of women piling sandbags in front of the first building on the edge of town. Gabe rode toward them and reined the dun again.

"What's going on?" he asked.

The women stopped their work and looked up at him. One was young and pretty, with blonde hair, wearing glasses. The others were older, their faces lined with care and hard work.

"Diablito's off the reservation!" one of the older women said, shielding her eyes with her hand.

"Who's Diablito?" he asked.

The women looked at him as if he was crazy. "You don't know who Diablito is?"

"No, ma'am."

"You must be new to these parts."

"As a matter of fact I am."

"Well you better find someplace to hide."

The women returned to their work with the sandbags. Gabe watched them with amusement, then rode down the main street of town. Everyone was busy building fortifications. Even children ran about, carrying rocks and adobe bricks. Men herded horses into barns. Shutters were pulled closed in front of the windows of houses.

Gabe saw a sign that said: LIVERY. He inclined the dun in that direction and rode through the opening of the building. It was cool and dim inside. A man stacked bales of hay in front of a window. Gabe dismounted and waited for the man to turn around, but the man didn't notice him.

"Howdy," Gabe said.

The man spun around. He had an egg-shaped bald head, and his eyes widened with fear at the sight of Gabe.

"Who're you?" the man asked.

"My name's Gabe Conrad. Can I get some grain for my horse?"

"Just put him in any stall. The grain's in the bin at the other end down there."

Gabe walked the dun into the stall and then made his way to the other end of the stable. He found the grain in a bin, and filled a bucket, bringing it back to the dun, setting it in front of him. Then he approached the man, who was heaving another bale of hay in front of the window.

"Hear you're having problems with the Apaches," Gabe said.

"Diablito's off the reservation," the man replied. "Won't be safe until they hunt him down and kill him."

"I just came across the desert from New Mexico, and I haven't seen any Apaches."

"Consider yourself lucky."

Gabe left the livery stable and looked up the street, seeing a sign that said: GENERAL STORE. He walked in that direction and approached a large squat adobe building with small windows. The sun was approaching midday, and its rays beat down fiercely on Gabe. The air was thick and hot. He'd been in the saddle since dawn, and felt stiff and hungry.

He entered the general store. Two men were inside, on opposite sides of the counter. One was buying shells for a shotgun. The man behind the counter wore a black mustache and long sideburns streaked with gray. He noticed Gabe and said: "Hello, stranger."

"Howdy," Gabe said. "I'll wait until you're finished."

"Where you comin' from?"

"New Mexico."

"Seen any Apaches?"

"Not a one."

"You were lucky."

"It was pretty quiet out there on the desert."

"Won't be for long."

Gabe sat at a table and rolled a cigarette. Nearby was a barrel of beans and a barrel of coffee. Shirts and pants hung from the rafters. Gabe lit the cigarette. The man who'd bought the shotgun shells paid for them and walked out of the store.

"My name's Barnes," said the man behind the counter. "What's your'n?"

"Gabe Conrad."

"When'd you get in town?"

"Just now."

"You come at a bad time. We're expectin' a visit from Diablito and his band. We got horses, ammunition and supplies, just what he's lookin' for. What can I do for you?"

"I need some supplies myself."

"Where you headed?"

"I was planning to go to Tucson."

"I think you'd better stay here until they hunt down Diablito. You won't stand a chance against him alone on the desert."

"You got something cold to drink?"

"Beer."

"How about sasparilla?"

"Don't have no sasparilla. You don't like whisky, I take it."

"No, I don't."

"Onliest other thing I've got is water."

"I'll take a glass of that if you don't mind."

Barnes worked the pump and poured a glass of water. Gabe took it and returned to the table. Another man entered the store and asked for shells for his rifle. Barnes placed a box of shells on the counter. The man turned around and saw Gabe. "Howdy," he said.

"Howdy."

"Don't reckon I seen you before."

"He just come to town," Barnes said.

"Across the desert alone?" the man asked Gabe.

"That's right."

"You was lucky to make it in one piece."

"That's what I was tellin' him," Barnes said.

The man carried his box of shells out of the general store.

"Who's this Diablito?" Gabe asked.

"The worst injun who ever lived," Barnes said.

"What's he done?"

"You name it—he done it. Murder, robbery, rape, stealin' horses. They shoulda strung him up while they had a chance, but no, they fed him and clothed him at the reservation. Now he's on the loose again. Just goes to show you—you can't trust an injun."

"Where's the reservation?"

"At Fort Jerome. About forty mile northeast of here."

A man and a woman entered the store together. The man

wanted ammunition and the woman needed to stock up on food. Barnes measured beans and cut salt pork, while Gabe watched and sipped his water. He wondered if Diablito was as bad as Barnes had said.

Gabe had been raised by the Sioux until he was fourteen, and understood the Indian point of view. Their ancestral lands were being taken away and they fought back as best they could against greater numbers and better equipment. The white man continually broke his promises to the Indian. Enticed to live on reservations, Indians frequently didn't get enough food, clothing or shelter. It was no wonder that they left and went on the warpath. Gabe knew he could never live on a reservation. For one thing, it would be far too boring.

The man and woman left with their goods. "Well, what can I do for you?" Barnes asked Gabe.

"I'll need some supplies," Gabe said. "Give me paper and a pencil and I'll write everything down."

"Here you go."

Barnes placed a sheet of paper and a pencil on the counter. Gabe arose and walked toward the counter, his boots clomping loudly on the floor. He towered over Barnes as he bent over the counter and wrote his order.

"When you want this stuff by?" Barnes asked.

"Soon as I can get it."

"You ain't plannin' on leavin' town, are you?"

"I was."

Barnes stared at Gabe in disbelief. "You must be crazy! Didn't I just tell you that Diablito's off the reservation? It ain't safe out there on the desert!"

"I didn't have any trouble when I was out there."

"You was lucky."

Gabe looked at Barnes and wondered if he and the whole town were overreacting. If Diablito was off the reservation, he was probably heading for Mexico where he'd be safe from the cavalry. Gabe had confidence in his ability to handle himself in the wilderness, but the desert wasn't the kind of wilderness to which he was accustomed. Maybe he'd better stay in Gleeson for awhile and see what developed.

"Is there a boarding house in town?" Gabe asked.

"You're in it."

"I'd like to get a room for the night, and my meals, and I'd like to take a bath."

Barnes cupped his hands around his mouth and shouted: "Martha!"

A few moments later a middle-aged woman appeared in a doorway at the rear of the store. "What is it?" she asked, pulling a stray hair out of her eyes.

"We've got a guest for the night, and he wants to take a bath."

"What's your name, stranger?" she asked.

"Gabe Conrad."

"I'm Martha Barnes. How do you do?"

Gabe shook her hand, and noticed the deep lines around her eyes. She was probably in her forties, but looked much older.

"Come with me," she said.

She led him down a dark cool corridor with a low ceiling, passing several other small rooms. A brightly colored Indian blanket decorated a wall of the corridor. Finally they came to a door and she opened it up.

"Here you go, Mister Conrad," she said.

Gabe entered the room. It wasn't much bigger than some jail cells he'd been in, and had a cot and a small dresser with a mirror and a wash basin.

"You said you wanted a bath?" she asked.

"Yes, ma'am, if you don't mind."

"Don't mind at all. You smell as if you could use a good bath, if you don't mind me sayin' so. I'll get Sally to draw the water for you. She's my daughter, and you'd best keep your hands off'n her, hear?"

"Yes, ma'am. While you're hunting down your daughter, I'll go out to the livery stable and get a change of clothes from my saddlebags. I hadn't intended to stay here in Gleeson, you see."

"This ain't no time to be out on the desert, young feller."

"That's what everybody tells me."

Gabe and Martha left the room, heading in different

directions. Gabe passed down the corridor and walked out of the general store, crossing the street and entering the stable, where he pulled the saddle off his horse.

"I'll be staying in town for awhile," he told the bald man who ran the stable. "Can I get my horse rubbed down?"

"I'll take care of it."

Gabe looked at the dun, who was eating grain out of a bucket. It'd be good for both of them to have a little rest. Gleeson wasn't much of a town, but it would be a welcome respite from the hot desert.

Gabe slung his saddlebags over his shoulder and returned to his room behind the general store. He sat on the cot and rolled himself a cigarette. As he was lighting it, there was a knock on the door.

"Come in!" he said.

The door opened and a young woman entered, carrying a tin tub. She was tall and well-built, with red hair that extended just below her ears. Her face had a wholesome look and her nose was slightly upturned. Gabe guessed that she was in her late teens.

She placed the tub in the middle of the floor. "I'll get the water now," she said.

"You must be Sally," he replied. "I'm Gabe."

"What're you doing in Gleeson?"

"Just passing through. You been living here long?"

"Most of my life."

"Doesn't seem to be much to do here."

"My mother and father keep me pretty busy."

They looked each other up and down for a few moments, then she said: "I'd better get the water now. You smell like a horse."

She walked out of the room, not bothering to close the door behind her. Gabe peeled off his shirt and looked at himself in the mirror on the dresser. His face and especially his neck were bronzed from the sun, and several days of whiskers had sprouted on his face. He could smell the odor from his body and it wasn't so pleasant.

Sally entered the room and poured two pitchers of hot water into the tub. Then she left. Gabe scooped some of the water into the wash basin and took his straight razor out of a saddlebag. He washed his face with soap and water and proceeded to shave. Meanwhile, Sally returned several times and emptied pitchers of water into the tub.

Gabe thought about Diablito. Although he was new to the Southwest, he'd heard about the depredations of the Apaches. They were supposed to be the poorest and most ferocious Indians in America, even worse than Commanches. He wondered how many Apaches had left the reservation with Diablito. Were there enough to attack a town like Gleeson? Gabe realized that a town with horses, food, and ammunition would be tempting to Apaches on the warpath.

Sally entered the room again and poured two more pitchers of water into the tub. "It's full now," she said.

"How'd you like to stay and wash my back?" he asked.

She smiled. "Don't be naughty."

Turning, she left the room and closed the door. Gabe finished shaving and took off his clothes. He sat in the tub and soaked for awhile, then scrubbed himself down.

Diablito had a broad thick chest and long muscular legs. His straight black hair was shoulder length and he wore a red strip of cloth around his head to keep his hair out of his eyes.

He lay on top of the hill and looked down at the ranch in the valley below. He was especially interested in the horses that congregated in the corral. Diablito's horses were tired. They'd been riding hard all day.

Black Hawk lay beside him, also looking at the ranch. Near them were other braves, all wearing breech clouts, with straight lines of red clay running across their cheeks and noses.

"We attack," Diablito said.

They crawled back to their horses in the chapparal nearby. The women and children were there, seeking shelter from the sun in the caves. Everyone was gaunt; rations had been short at Fort Jerome.

The Apache braves mounted their horses. Diablito's eyes were cold and hard. He had a rifle and a bow with a quiver of arrows, but not much ammunition.

"We go!" he told his braves.

They wheeled their horses around and charged down the side of the hill. Then they raced across the desert to the ranch, whooping and yelling, brandishing their weapons. At the ranch, white men and women ran for shelter, hollering that Apaches were coming. Diablito cracked a grim smile.

The Apaches swooped across the desert and headed toward the ranch. A fusillade of gunfire erupted from the ranch house. Diablito heard bullets whistle past him and felt elated. It was good for a warrior to be on the attack again.

The Apaches thundered toward the ranch house. When they got close, they dismounted and ran forward on foot. Some of them fired their rifles at the ranch house, others shot arrows through the windows. A group of Apaches with hatchets charged the front door, while others circled around and covered the back door.

Diablito was with the braves at the front door, hacking it down with hatchets. Other Apaches dived through the windows of the house. There were screams and much gunfire inside. Finally the door splintered. Red Sleeves charged it and broke through, but a bullet hit him in the chest and knocked him down. Diablito jumped through the opening in the door, and saw a white man with a beard in front of him, loading a Sharps rifle.

Diablito hurled his hatchet at the white man, and the blade of the hatchet buried itself in his chest. The white man coughed blood and dropped to his knees. Diablito rushed forward and pulled his hatchet out of the white man's chest.

The Apaches were in the main room of the ranch house. Diablito jumped on top of a table, then hurled himself at another white man pointing a pistol at Black Hawk. The white man became aware of Diablito at the last moment and turned to face him, but he was too late. Diablito split his head open with the hatchet, and the white man fell to the floor.

In a corner, Spider Arms was stabbling another white man. The other white men in the room were dead. A woman cowered in the corner, tears streaming down her eyes, her hands trembling. She tried to scream but no sound came out of her mouth.

Torrés approached her and smiled. The woman pushed her shoulder into the corner. Then her eyes became white and she fainted onto the floor.

"Take her," Diablito said. "Get all the guns. Look for food."

He walked down the passageway and opened a door. A boy of eight or nine hid behind his bunk bed, pointing a pistol at Diablito. Diablito ducked, and the bullet fired over his head. Laughing, Diablito dived on the boy and pulled the pistol out of his hands.

"You will come with us," Diablito said to the boy, who squirmed in his grasp.

Apache braves carried the woman and boy to the horses. Other Apaches carried sacks of flour and beans from the kitchen. A group of Apaches set fire to the house and barn, and flames licked up the walls. More Apaches opened the gates to the corral and let the horses out, herding them toward the mountains.

Diablito jumped onto a fresh horse and dug his heels into its ribs. He and the other Apaches rode away, carrying their captives and booty. Some of the Apaches herded the stolen horses, tied together with stolen rope.

They were looking forward to the feast of horsemeat they'd have that night. It would be their first good meal since they agreed to go to the reservation more than two years ago.

It was evening in Gleeson. Gabe sat at a round table in the dining room of Jake Barnes' home, as Martha Barnes placed a thick steak on the plate in front of him. He was seated between Martha and young Sally, and occasionally his knees touched Sally's underneath the tablecloth.

"Where you from?" Barnes asked Gabe. "Hope you won't think I'm nosy or anythin' like that, but we don't get strangers here in Gleeson very often."

"I'm from up in Montana," Gabe said.

"What're you doin' in these parts?"

"Just moseying along."

"Lookin' for work?"

"Nope."

Barnes wanted to ask how Gabe got his money, because Gabe seemed to be well-heeled, but figured that'd be too personal a question. Meanwhile, Martha passed Gabe the bowl of mashed potatoes, and Gabe scooped some out with a spoon. When he passed the bowl to Sally, their eyes met.

"You said you're headed for Tucson?" Barnes asked.

"That's right."

"You got folks there?"

"Nope."

Barnes looked him in the eye. "You ain't wanted by the law, are you?"

"Nope, are you?"

Barnes laughed. "Hell no!"

Gabe cut into his steak. "Tell me about Diablito."

"He's a thievin', murderin' son of a bitch," Barnes replied. "Never was any good and never will be any good. I knew he wouldn't stay on the reservation long. He ain't happy unless he's killin' a white man."

"Well," said Gabe, "it's hard for Indians to live on reservations. They're used to roaming free on their land."

"You sound like one of them Indian lovers from the East, the kind who ain't never set eyes on an Indian in their lives, but somehow know all about 'em."

"Jake!" said Martha, a tone of admonishment in her voice. "Don't talk to our guest that way."

"Waal, I'm sorry," Barnes said, "but if there's anything I hate, it's an injun lover. Next thing you know, he'll be lecturin' us on injun culture. As far as I'm concerned, the injuns never had a culture. The only thing they ever learned how to do is build a bonfire."

Gabe chuckled. "I understand how you feel."

"Look at how the injuns live," Barnes continued. "The men sit around all day and let the wimmin do all the work. Once in a while the men get up off their asses and go huntin'. Then they come back and the wimmin have to skin the dead animals and cook 'em, while the men take it easy. I tell you, the sooner all the injuns around here are dead, the better."

"They're just fighting for their land," Gabe said.

"Is that so? Waal, land belongs to the man who can take it and hold it. It ain't gonna be their land for long."

"I know," Gabe said.

His knee touched Sally's again, and he wondered if she was doing it on purpose. He glanced at her, and she was placing a forkful of beans into her mouth. Her skin was smooth and lovely in the light of the kerosene lamp flickering in the middle of the table.

"Are you married?" Mrs. Barnes asked Gabe.

"No, ma'am."

"Ever been married?"

"No, ma'am."

"How come a good-lookin' man like you's never been married?"

"Don't know, ma'am."

Sally blushed. "Mother!"

"Just askin'." Mrs. Barnes turned to Gabe again. "You oughtta think about settlin' down. Don't wanna be a saddle bum all your life, do you?"

"Mother!"

"Shush, Sally. I'm only havin' a civil conversation with our guest." She looked at Gabe again. "Do you wanna be a saddle bum all your life?"

"No, ma'am."

"Awful nice little town we got here. We could use another hand helpin' out here at the store."

Gabe saw himself as a storekeeper, and nearly gagged on his steak. Sally saw the expression on his face and burst out laughing.

Her mother stared at her. "What're you laughin' at, girl?"

"Nothin'."

"Watch your manners."

"Yes, ma'am."

Gabe placed some mashed potatoes into his mouth. Sally's knee touched his again and he felt himself becoming aroused. She was a very appealing young woman, strong and graceful at the same time. He imagined how her smooth white skin looked underneath her dress.

• • •

It appeared to be a solid wall of rock in the distance, but Diablito and his band rode straight toward it on their fresh horses. The Apaches were in high spirits, for their raid had been successful. They had meat and beans and had taken captives. They were free from the routine and shame of the reservation. It felt good to be free again.

The wall of the mountain range came closer, as the molten red sun sank toward the horizon. Birds flew out of holes in tall cactuses as they approached. Diablito rode in front of his band, feeling like a warrior chief again, instead of a beggar.

He knew that hard times were ahead. The blue coats would hunt them like animals, and if he headed south into Mexico, the Mexican cavalry would try to surround him.

Life would be hazardous, but it could be no other way for an Apache. Better to die a warrior than starve slowly like a rat. Diablito was happy with his decision to leave the reservation. He would make the *White Eyes* pay for all the humiliation they'd inflicted upon him these past two years.

They approached the side of the mountain, and still it appeared like one solid wall. Then as they drew closer, they veered to the left. From that angle they could see that the mountain in that area wasn't one solid wall, but two mountains, one slightly in front of the other. Between the both of them was a passageway wide enough for three horsemen abreast. It was an old Apache hideout, and the white eyes had never known of its existence.

Diablito slowed as he approached the entrance. Then, sitting erectly on his horse, he rode into it. His band followed him into a basin surrounded with mountains and covered with grass. There was no other entrance to the basin and no way out except over the mountains. At the far end was a gorge with a stream and a small lake. Mescal, nopal, and other food-bearing plants grew in the basin. Apaches could exist here for a long period of time.

Diablito rode toward the small lake, looking around at the familiar cliffs and ledges. He'd been here many times over the years. It was like coming home. Behind him, the men and women in his band murmured their approval. All were glad to be off the reservation and back to their ancestral lands.

Diablito came to the lake and dismounted. He led his horse forward and let him drink. The other Apaches did the same. Diablito stood with his legs apart and his hands clasped behind his back. They would be safe here for awhile.

Diablito turned around. "Black Hawk, post your guards!" he ordered.

Black Hawk called four guards and told them to climb the mountain and watch the desert for blue coat columns. Meanwhile, the women gathered the type of wood that didn't make smoke when it burned. Diablito walked back to the young boy he'd captured.

"Get down from your horse!" Diablito ordered.

Terrified, the boy climbed down and stood in front of Diablito, trembling all over.

"What is your name?" Diablito asked.

"Phillip Jones," the boy stuttered.

"Go to the women," Diablito said. "They will tell you what to do."

Gabe swallowed his last drop of coffee.

"Another piece of pie?" asked Martha Barnes.

"No thank you, ma'am. I'm full. I think I'll go outside and have a smoke."

Jake Barnes stared at him. "Are you crazy! Do you want one of them Apaches to sneak up on you and cut your damn fool throat?"

"I won't go that far away," Gabe said.

"You won't have to go that far away. We've had Apaches come right into town at night and steal things."

"I'll be all right," Gabe told him.

"Damn fool."

Gabe excused himself and walked down the corridor to his room. He put on his hat and then went outside via the back entrance of the building. He saw the privy and a few sheds, and beyond them was the night desert.

A half moon hung in a sky in which billions of stars were ablaze. The moon was on the horizon, casting long shadows of cactus and chapparal. Gabe walked beyond the sheds and sat on a rock, lighting his cigarette. He knew that Sioux Indians didn't usually attack at night, and figured Apaches were the same.

He puffed his cigarette and watched the stars twinkle in the sky. The Barnes family were nice people, and Sally was quite beautiful, but he thought he'd leave tomorrow. The town was awfully small and he felt cooped up.

He thought of Jake Barnes' comments about Indians. Gabe had heard similar sentiments from other white men during his travels across the frontier. The white men didn't understand they were stealing land that belonged to somebody else, and the Indians didn't realize they were in the path of a great expanding nation. Both sides had to fight for what they considered rightfully theirs, and both sides looked upon each other as criminals. It was a problem that had no solution, and Gabe was in the middle because he'd had white parents, but the Sioux Indians had raised him.

He heard a twig crackle behind him, and dropped silently to the ground, pulling out his Colt pistol. Sally emerged from the darkness. "Gabe?" she said softly.

He stood and holstered his Colt. "I'm over here."

"What were you doing on the ground?"

"I thought you might be an Apache."

"Could you roll me a cigarette?"

"Have a seat."

She sat on the rock and crossed her legs. He sat beside her and rolled a cigarette.

"Your momma know you're here?" he asked.

"She thinks I'm in my room."

He passed her the cigarette, then struck a match on the rock and held it up. She puffed the cigarette until it glowed cherry red.

"Thank you," she said.

"I bet your daddy would give you a spanking if he knew you were here."

"I bet he would too." She turned away from him and gazed at the desert. "It's so beautiful out here, and so frightening at the same time. The rattlesnakes come out at night, and the scorpions, and lizards, too. I wish I could leave this place."

"Where would you like to go?"

"Anywhere."

"Anywhere covers a lot of ground."

"Tucson would be okay, I guess. That's where you're headed, isn't it?"

"Yes, but I don't suppose it's any place for a single woman."

"I'm sure I could find a decent job. I can read and write and do arithmetic, you know. Sometimes I think I'd rather do anything than stay another day in Gleeson. I'm so bored I could die. There's nothing to do here but the chores. I see the same people day in and day out. Once in a blue moon a stranger shows up like you, and it's a major event."

He puffed his cigarette in the darkness. "I know what you mean. I don't want to stay here, either."

"But you have to stay here, because Diablito is off the reservation. It's dangerous on the desert. It's even dangerous here in town."

"We'll see."

"What do you mean by that?"

"I think I'll leave in the morning."

"That's crazy!"

"Maybe."

She narrowed her eyes and looked at him. "Who are you, anyway?"

"I already told you—my name's Gabe Conrad."

"But I mean—who are you really? What do you do? What's your purpose in life?"

"I just live, that's all. I have no great ambitions."

"I wish I could be like you," she said. "You're free to go wherever you want, but I'm stuck here in Gleeson."

"I guess we have to accept the hand we're dealt, and make the best of it."

"I hate it here," she said.

"Things could always be worse," he told her. "You could be a captive in Diablito's camp right now."

She smiled wryly. "Yes, I suppose that'd be worse than this."

He looked at her. She was slim and lovely in the moonlight,

wearing a thin cotton dress. He wanted to take her in his arms and feel her young body against his, but she was only a girl, full of dreams and innocence. He could offer her no future. There was no point starting something that wouldn't go anywhere. He didn't want to make her more unhappy than she already was.

Out on the desert, at the mouth of a cave, Diablito sat in a circle with the elders and principal warriors of his band, smoking a cigarette rolled from special leaves, herbs and spices. The medicine man, Cibicue, wore his ceremonial buckskin cap decorated with raven feathers, and prayed to *Ussen*, the Apache God.

The Apaches passed the cigarette to each other, while Cibicue gazed at the heavens and murmured weird incantations. The contents of Cibicue's medicine bag were arranged in front of him, the quartz crystals, cattail pollen, herbs, red ocher, and the dried head of a small bird lying on the sand.

The cigarette was long and fat, and its smoke curled into the air. The smoke was making Diablito feel light-headed and strange. He was mildly hallucinating, seeing spirits and animals in the sky.

A fire glowed in the middle of the circle of warriors. Diablito looked down at it, and it was like blood. Diablito had seen much blood in his day. The life of an Apache was a life of violence. When he was a boy, he'd never known that a person could die of natural causes.

He'd fought the Mexicans and now he was fighting the white eyes. There seemed to be no end of fighting. The old men told legends of a time when the Apaches had lived at peace, but that had been long ago. There could be no peace with the white eyes, because the white eyes lied so much.

Once there had been an honest white eye. He was Gray Wolf, the great white eye warrior who was known as General Crook among his people. He had not spoken with a forked tongue, but he was gone now, replaced by liars and cheats.

Cibicue finished his prayers to Ussen. Everyone looked to Diablito, for it was his turn to speak. Diablito felt as if he was floating a few inches above the ground.

"My warriors," he said. "We are engaged in a great struggle for survival. The odds are against us, but Ussen protects the brave. We must fight the white eyes until either we or they are all dead. They give us no choice. This is a war that they want, a war they force us to fight. It is better to die with honor than live with shame. I know all of you well, and all of you know me. I will not fail you, and you will not fail me. Tomorrow we ride. We must show no mercy, because the white eyes show no mercy to us. They have tried to starve us to death. They have withheld clothing and blankets in the winter so we would freeze to death. They want us to leave our sacred ancestral lands and live in foreign places where we will weaken and die. They have broken each and every one of their promises. They are the devils of the earth. We must oppose them. That is my opinion." Diablito paused. The smoke was making him feel euphoric. "Are you with me, my brothers?" he asked.

There was silence for a few moments, then Black Hawk raised his hand. "I am with you," he said.

"I, too," added Spider Arms.

"And I," said He Who Runs Fast.

The others raised their hands and gave their approval. Diablito could feel the energy from their bodies pass into his. He smiled and held out his arms to them.

"It is good," he said. *"Enjuh."*

Gabe took off his clothes and crawled into bed. He placed his Colt underneath the pillow and pulled up the sheet and blanket.

It was cool in the room. The temperature had dropped drastically from what it had been at midday. He was learning that the desert was a place of extremes. He wasn't sure whether he liked it or not.

He'd made up his mind that he'd leave in the morning. Gleeson was a ramshackle little town and Sally had been right: there was nothing to do. Gabe was willing to take his chances alone on the desert. He was confident he could handle any problem that might crop up.

He thought of Sally and her tall lissome body. He wanted to make love to her, but she was a sweet girl and he didn't want to take advantage of her. But her skin was so smooth and delicate. Her eyes were oval and pale blue. She was beautiful now, but a few years of loneliness and hard work in a desert town would put deep lines in those smooth cheeks. She'd become grouchy and rough. Finally she'd get desperate and marry the most convenient man.

Gabe rolled over and fluffed up his pillow. He closed his eyes and tried to sleep, but couldn't. Occasionally he met a woman who really moved him, and Sally was that kind of woman. He couldn't understand why she affected him so profoundly. She was pretty, but so were a lot of other women who didn't move him at all. What special quality did she have? Gabe couldn't figure it out. "Women," he muttered.

He felt agitated. The bed was soft but somehow he couldn't get comfortable. He decided to get up and smoke one last cigarette. Then he heard something. There were footsteps outside his door. He grabbed his pistol and bounded out of bed, crouching naked in the corner.

There was a light tapping on his door. He crouched silently in the corner, and heard the tapping again. Moving silently along the wall, he reached the door and unlatched it. The door opened and Sally stood in the passageway, wearing a baggy white cotton nightdress.

"Can I come in?" she asked, an expression of terror on her face.

"What's wrong?"

"I want to talk with you."

"Just a moment. Let me put on my pants."

He pulled his pants off the chair and stepped into the legs. She entered the room. It was dark; they could barely see each other. He closed the door and latched it.

"What do you want?" he asked.

A tremor passed over her, then she said: "I want you to make love to me."

He stared at her for a few moments. She looked as though she might faint.

"I think you'd better sit down," he said.

She sat at the edge of the bed and looked up hopefully at him.

He stood with his back to the adobe wall and wondered what to do. She was a tasty morsel, a terrific temptation. But she was no more than a kid.

"How old are you?" he asked.

"Eighteen."

"You're not lying, are you?"

"No."

"I'm very flattered that you've come to me this way, but I'm just an old saddle bum and tomorrow I'm moving on, no matter what happens here tonight."

"I don't care," she said.

"You should get married to some nice man and have children."

"I don't want any of the men in this town. I only want you."

"You won't have any future with me."

"I don't have any future without you either, so what's the difference?"

Gabe was perplexed. He didn't know what to do, and when he didn't know what to do he always thought it best to smoke a cigarette and think things over. He moved toward his shirt to get his bag of tobacco, and she arose from the bed, intercepting him, standing only a few inches away.

"Where are you going?" she asked.

"To get my tobacco out of my shirt."

"Don't you like me?"

"Yes, I like you."

"But you don't think I'm pretty."

"I think you're very pretty."

"Then why don't you make love to me? Is there anything wrong with you? Are you one of those men who don't like girls?"

"No, I like girls."

"Well?"

He looked her in the eye. "You're being awfully brazen, young lady."

"I don't care."

She took a step forward, and her body touched his lightly. He could feel her young pert breasts against his chest. The blood began to pound in his neck. To hell with the tobacco and to hell with everything else.

He wrapped his arms around her waist. She placed her hands on his shoulders. They looked into each other's eyes. He could feel her body trembling against him, and new strength filled him.

"You're asking for it," he said.

"I know it," she replied.

Lost in her youth and beauty, he hugged her to him. She raised her face and he kissed her lips. She dug her fingernails into his shoulders and her breath came in gasps. He picked her up and carried her to the bed, laying her down gently.

"Have you ever done this before?" he asked.

"No."

He lay beside her and cupped her breast as he kissed her ear. She closed her eyes and sighed softly. Their lips met and he slipped his tongue into her mouth. She moaned and squirmed underneath him. She still wore her thin cotton nightgown, and he had on only his jeans. They hugged and kissed for several minutes, and the flame between them grew brighter.

He raised his head and looked down at her. The features of her face were dim and indistinct, but her eyes glowed like coals.

"Take off my gown," she whispered.

He wasn't going to argue with her. It was too late for that. He'd passed the point of no return. Kneeling on the bed, he slowly lifted the hem of her nightgown. She raised her body so he could move it up. Inch by inch, her young supple body was revealed in all its splendor. Her legs were long and sinuous, her hips were narrow and her belly flat. He continued to raise the nightgown, and her firm proud breasts came into view.

Gabe bent over and kissed one of the nipples. Sally ran her fingers through his long hair and pulled his head more tightly against her. Her body smelled like a flower, and she tasted like candy. Gabe thought he was going mad. He pulled the nightgown over her head and threw it across the room. Then he took off his pants.

He lay on top of her, and she shivered. He pulled the covers over them and hugged her tightly against him. Their lips met again and their tongues engaged in soft combat. He moved his hands down her body and felt her butt. It was muscular and gently curved. Gabe's pulse was pounding. She scratched her fingernails across his back and bit his lip.

He knew that young girls were sweet and cute until you got in bed with them, and then they went totally beserk. The only thing to do was hold on. It was like riding a wild horse. They were interlocked together now, moving wildly. She had enthusiasm but no finesse, but who needed finesse?

Out on the desert, a coyote howled at the moon.

It was the middle of the night. Diablito sat alone on top of the mountain, smoking another ceremonial *cigarito*. The night desert stretched out for miles beneath him, all the way to the horizon. He saw flat land, valleys, mountains and buttes, weird and eerie in the moonlight. To his left was Fort Jerome, and he saw a few lights twinkling in the darkness. On his right was the town of Gleeson, also with some lights twinkling. He made out the shapes of ranches and trails with his sharp eyes.

There was a time when only Apaches were in this country, and there hadn't been that many Apaches. The country had been wild and free, abundant with plant food and wild game. Now it was a battle ground, and the Apaches were the ones being hunted like wild animals.

All an Apache could hope for was to die like a warrior. That was the gift that Diablito intended to give his braves. It would be disgraceful to die of starvation or old age on a filthy, crowded reservation.

Diablito looked up at the starry heavens. Why was *Ussen* making the Apaches suffer so? Why had he sent the white eyes to despoil the land? Diablito shook his head. There was no way of knowing what *Ussen* wanted. All a warrior could do was die with honor.

The white eyes would pay for what they'd inflicted upon the Apaches. Diablito would see to that. The white eyes were no good to the marrow of their bones. All they could do was lie and cheat, and the few good ones among them, like Gray Wolf, were greatly outnumbered by the wicked ones.

They would learn that they couldn't lie and cheat with impunity. Perhaps *Ussen* was using Diablito to punish the white eyes for their thievery and trickery. Diablito would teach the white eyes a few lessons. They would pay a high price for all they had done.

Diablito yawned. He was getting tired. Smoking the cigarito to the end, he stood and stretched on top of the mountain, holding out his arms as if embracing the entire desert.

Then he descended the mountain, heading toward the caves. He passed one of the guards sitting next to a rock. Diablito nodded to the guard, and the guard nodded back. Diablito and his band had to stay alert at all times. They couldn't let the blue coats sneak up on them.

He made his way back to the valley and approached the small lake at the end of the canyon. Kneeling beside the water, he cupped some in his hands and raised it to his lips. He and his tribe always believed this water was sacred, that it flowed from the very heart of *Ussen*.

He heard something. It wasn't an animal and it wasn't an Apache, because animals and Apaches didn't make so much noise. Diablito rose to his knees and looked around. Something was moving through the underbrush. He drew his knife and stalked silently toward it. The creature, or whatever it was, stopped and moved, stopped and moved, making a terrific racket. What could it be? The guards were high on the mountains and at the mouth of the canyon. What was here at that time of night?

Diablito crawled through the underbrush, his knife in his teeth. He heard the creature move ahead of him, and saw something move. Diablito angled to the side to cut the creature off. He moved across the desert swiftly and silently, then paused behind a tall cactus plant and waited.

The creature came closer. Diablito knew by now that it was a person, and guessed who it must be. He waited until the person came closer, then stepped out from behind the cactus plant.

Phillip Jones stood before him, his eyes bulging with horror at the sight of Diablito, who laughed. The boy turned to run, and Diablito swooped down on him, lifting him up by the scruff of his neck and turning him around to look into his face.

The boy had a thin sallow face and a shock of curly black hair. He kicked his feet in the air and Diablito laughed at him.

"I hate you!" the boy said. "You killed my father!"

"I am your father now," Diablito replied.

Gabe and Sally lay in each other's arms, breathing heavily from their exertions. Their bodies were plastered against each other with perspiration, and they were exhausted.

"You'd better go back to your room now," Gabe said.

"Just a little while longer," she replied.

"You don't want your father to catch you."

"He won't catch me—don't worry."

Just then Gabe heard something on the other side of the door. He reached underneath the pillow for his pistol, just as the sound of a terrific explosion rent the air. The door blew apart, and Gabe jumped out of bed. Jake Barnes stepped through the shattered, smoking ruin of the door, carrying a shotgun, followed by his wife Martha. Sally screamed and covered herself with sheet and blanket. Gabe pointed his pistol at Barnes, who aimed his shotgun at Gabe. Both men glowered at each other.

"So that's the way it is!" boomed Jake Barnes. "You show a man a little hospitality and he takes advantage of it!"

Martha stomped toward the bed and whacked her daughter across the top of the head. "You little slut!"

Gabe focused his eyes on Jake Barnes' trigger finger. If it moved, Gabe would fire his pistol first.

"You'd better put that shotgun down," Gabe said, "unless you're gonna use it."

"I oughta blow your damned head off!"

"Drop the shotgun, or make your play."

Jake Barnes looked at the armed naked man in front of him, but Jake Barnes was no gunfighter. He was angry about his daughter being found in bed with a man, but he wasn't about to die for it.

"I'm not going to tell you again," Gabe said.

Jake Barnes dropped the shotgun to the floor. Gabe put on his pants. Martha Barnes slapped her daughter in the face again. "You oughta be ashamed of yourself."

Sally jumped out of bed, and she was stark naked. She had a red mark on her breast where Gabe had kissed her too passionately for too long. Staring defiantly at her mother and father, she dropped her nightgown over her head.

"Waal," said Jake Barnes to his daughter, "if you're old enough to sleep with strangers, you're old enough to leave home." Jake Barnes turned to Gabe. "You git out, too. You done wore out your welcome."

"Now just a second," Gabe said, holstering his pistol. "Let's not get all worked up over nothing. You can't throw your daughter out onto the desert."

"Can't I?" Jake Barnes said.

He picked up his shotgun and walked out the door. Martha scowled at her daughter.

"Whore!" he said.

Martha followed her husband out the door, leaving Gabe and Sally alone in the room. A tear rolled down Sally's cheek. Gabe walked to her and placed his hands on her shoulders.

"Don't worry," he said. "They'll get over it."

"No they won't," Sally said. "They're awfully hard people."

"I'll have a talk with them in the morning."

"It won't do no good."

Gabe sat on the bed and put on his stockings. "Guess I'd better find someplace else to spend the night."

"Me, too."

"This is your home. You don't have to leave."

"Oh, yes I do. My Daddy threw me out. Didn't you hear him?"

"He didn't really mean it."

"Yes he did."

"I'm sure he'll cool off by morning."

"Oh, no he won't."

"Then what will you do?"

"I don't know. Where are you going?"

"To the stable."

"I guess that's where I'll go too."

"I don't think you should leave your home."

She stared at him coldly through her tears. "Why don't you just come out and say it."

"Come out and say what?"

"That you don't want me to go with you."

"I just think you'd be better off at home with your family."

"They just threw me out."

"They'll change their minds."

She pinched her lips together in pain and anger, then said: "You wish they'd change their minds, because you don't want to be with me anymore. You really don't care about me at all."

"That's not true."

"Yes it is, and you know it. Why don't you be honest and admit it like a man."

She sat on the bed and sobbed, covering her face in her hands. Gabe looked at her, his heart sinking in his breast. He sat beside her and placed his arm around her shoulders, but she threw it off.

"Get away from me!" she said bitterly.

"Don't be that way," he said gently. "You know that I care about you. I'm just a little surprised by what happened, that's all."

"You really don't care about me."

"Yes I do."

"If you cared about me, you wouldn't ask me to stay here with my parents."

"You're just a young girl. You belong with your parents."

"They don't think so. Besides, what happened here'll be all over town by morning. I can't live here anymore. I'm leaving with you or without you."

"Do you have a horse?"

"No."

"Then how're you gonna leave?"

"I'll walk."

"You won't get far on the desert."

"I'll worry about that."

"What if Diablito gets you."

"I'd be better off dead than stuck in this town, with parents who don't give a damn about me."

"I keep telling you that they'll get over it."

"Maybe they will, but I won't." She raised her head proudly. "I'm a woman now. If you won't take me with you, I'll find somebody else."

"Who?"

"I don't know yet."

She raised the hem of her gown and daubed the tears from her face. Then her body was wracked by another paroxysm of sobbing. Gabe felt sorry for her. She was so young and pretty, and in such a jam.

"Listen," he said softly, "I'd like to help you, but I don't know what to do."

She raised her tear-stained face. "Just take me with you to the first big town we come to. Then I'll be on my own."

"What will you do?"

"I already told you I can read and write and do arithmetic. I'll find a job in a store someplace, and if I can't do that, I'll be a dance hall girl. If I can't survive one way, I'll survive another way—you can bet your bottom dollar on that. You won't have to worry about me, if that's what you're thinking about."

He couldn't help admiring her spunk. She was a strong, healthy girl. He didn't blame her for wanting to leave that little town. Her parents would make life awfully difficult for her if she stayed. They didn't seem to be the most understanding people in the world. Gabe thought Sally seemed like the kind of person who could make her way all right in the world if somebody just gave her a chance.

"Look at me," he said.

She raised her face and looked at him with swollen bloodshot eyes.

"I'll take you with me," he told her, "but you have to do whatever I say. I'm going to be the boss, get it?"

A smile creased her pretty face. "I get it."

"If you give me any trouble, we're finished, understand?"

"I understand."

"It might get tough out there, and if it does, you'll have to carry your own weight. I may not be able to take care of you every minute."

"Don't worry—I can take care of myself."

"And just remember one thing: first big town we come to, we're splitting up. That's our agreement, right?"

"Right."

He held out his hand. At first she didn't know what he wanted, but then she figured it out. Feeling awkward, she shook hands with him the way she imagined men shook hands.

"It's a deal," she said.

# CHAPTER TWO

It was morning, and Gabe entered the general store. "I've come to pick up my supplies," he said.

"Got 'em for you right here," replied Jake Barnes coldly.

Gabe checked the goods on the counter: salt pork, canned beans, coffee, biscuits, honey and tobacco. Gabe and Jake Barnes behaved civilly with each other. No one would ever guess that they'd been aiming guns at each other only a few hours ago.

"I'll also need a Colt revolver with a belt and holster, and a Winchester rifle," Gabe said. "Plus a few boxes of ammunition for each.

Jake Barnes looked at him curiously. He knew Gabe already had a pistol and rifle, and wondered what he wanted more for. Then he realized the answer. Gabe was arming his daughter for the long trek across the desert. Jake Barnes took down a rifle from the wall and placed it on the counter, then opened a drawer and took out a pistol. He wanted to shoot Gabe with it, but didn't dare try.

"How much?" Gabe asked.

Jake Barnes told him, and Gabe paid. Then Gabe packed the food inside his saddlebags. He tossed the saddlebags over his shoulder, picking up the other equipment, and walked outside, where Sally was waiting on the sidewalk, a bulging carpetbag beside her. She wore blue jeans, boots, a white canvas shirt, and a light brown cowboy hat with a flat brim.

"You look like you're ready for the trail," Gabe told her.

"I am."

She looked nervous, and Gabe thought that was reasonable, because she was leaving home for the first time. Her eyes were large and slightly slanted, and her jaw was set firmly. She was trying to be brave. Gabe hoped she wouldn't make any more problems for him than she'd made already.

He held out the new pistol. "You ever shoot one of these?" he asked.

"A few times."

"How about this?" He showed her the Winchester.

"I know how to shoot a rifle. Everybody around here learns, because of the Apaches."

"Strap on the pistol," he said, "and hope that you never have to use it."

She took the gunbelt and tied it around her waist low like a gunfighter.

"We might as well get going," he said. "Here, carry this."

He handed her some of the supplies, and they carried their loads across the street to the livery stable, where Gabe bought a horse and saddle for her, with a boot for the Winchester. She was silent and solemn as he buckled on the saddle and lashed her carpetbag behind it. Then he saddled his own horse and slung his saddlebags over it. He paid the man in the livery stable his bill.

"Time to get going," he said to Sally.

"I appreciate what you're doing for me," she said. "I'll pay you back someday. I promise."

He nodded, although he didn't expect her to ever pay him back. It was just the breaks of the trail. He climbed on the dun and she raised herself onto her horse, an apaloosa. The man who owned the livery stable looked at them curiously as they rode out onto the street.

No one was in sight, but Gabe could see faces watching from behind windows and curtains. The gossip probably was all over town. Sally had slept with a man and her folks had thrown her out.

They rode down the main street of the tiny town, aware of all the eyes on them. No eyes watched from the windows of the general store. Jake Barnes and Martha were somewhere in their back rooms, evidently.

Gabe looked at Sally, and she was holding her head high, jouncing up and down in her saddle. She looked strong, healthy and determined, not soft and dainty like some women. Gabe felt drawn to her. He looked forward to camping out with her that night in some remote little corner of the desert.

"How do you feel?" he said to her.

"Good," she replied.

They came to the edge of town. Two small boys were standing beside the road, looking up at them.

"Goodbye, Sally," one of them said.

"So long, Mortimer."

Ahead was the desert. The sky was cloudless and it looked as though it was going to be another simmering day. Tall Saguaro cactus plants covered the desert like soldiers, and high overhead three buzzards circled lazily in the sky.

"Keep your eyes open," Gabe told her. "We're in Apache country now."

She didn't reply. He glanced sideways at her, imagining what she must be going through. She was leaving home for the first time in her life, with a man she hardly knew. She was probably a little scared.

The town of Gleeson receded into the distance behind them until it disappeared behind hills and phalanxes of cactus plants. Gabe's sharp eyes roved from side to side as he scanned the desert ahead for signs of Apaches. He didn't want to ride into a trap.

The sun rose in the sky and the day became hotter. Gabe's perspiration soaked into his light cotton shirt. He turned to Sally and saw that she had stained her armpits. Dots of perspiration were on her face, which had taken on a bronze glow.

"How're you holding up?" he asked.

"Okay."

She looked sexy, rocking back and forth in her saddle. Her legs were long and strong. There was nothing frail about her, but there was nothing masculine about her either. She was the kind of frontier woman who could raise a family, cook meals, and perform arduous household chores from sunup to sundown without a whimper. Gabe looked forward more and more to camping out with her that night. She was simple and straightforward, but yet quite beautiful at the same time.

"Getting tired?" he asked.

"Nope, are you?"

He smiled, knowing she wouldn't admit being tired even if she was. She was determined to be strong, and that would make her strong.

At midmorning Gabe spotted movement to his right, several miles away across the trackless desert. He stopped the dun and turned in his saddle, peering in that direction.

"What is it?" she asked.

He didn't say anything as he narrowed his eyes, trying to perceive what was there. Focusing intensely, he made out the forms of three seminaked riders moving across the desert in a direction roughly parallel to the one he was taking. They were Indians, probably Apaches. Gabe knew that if he could see them, they also were aware of him, but they just loped along on their horses as if they didn't care about him.

"What's out there?" Sally asked.

"Apaches."

She froze in her saddle. "You're kidding."

"No, I'm not."

"Are there many of them."

"Only three, but they're not headed in this direction."

She wiped her mouth with the back of her hand. Gabe could see that she was concerned.

"Scared?" he asked.

"A little."

"I'll take you back to Gleeson if you want."

She thought about it for a few moments. "No thanks."

"Getting homesick?"

"Not at all."

He rode closer to her and smiled. "I think you're a wonderful woman."

"You didn't kiss me this morning. I didn't know what you thought."

"I didn't kiss you because it would've been awkward in that town with everybody looking."

"There's nobody around right now," she said.

He bent sideways in his saddle and touched his lips to hers. She poked her tongue out slightly, and it tasted like a rosebud. Gabe leaned back to his upright position in the saddle, his heart racing.

"We've got to get going," he said. "Got to cover as much ground as we can."

They moved out again. Gabe looked in the direction where he'd seen the Apaches, but they were gone. He was annoyed at himself for not noticing where they'd disappeared. If he'd been alone he would've kept his eyes on them, but he'd let Sally distract him. He didn't know whether to be annoyed with himself or annoyed with her.

"What's the matter?" she asked.

"I don't see those Apaches anymore."

"I hope they've gone away."

Gabe knew how unpredictable Indians could be, because he knew all their tricks, or at least the tricks of the Sioux who'd raised him. Indians were masters of deception. Those Apaches out there could be headed toward a specific destination, or they could be searching for someone to ambush.

The sun became a pan of silver radiating intense heat out of the sky. The heat reflected off the desert sand and Gabe felt as though he was in an oven. The air he breathed in was warm, and it dried out his nasal passages. His throat became parched. Unwrapping his canteen strap from the pommel on the saddle, he took a swig. He hoped he'd soon find a water hole for the horses.

He and Sally continued their trek across the desert. They were transversing gently rolling ground that seemed to go on forever. Birds were everywhere, flying from cactus flower to cactus flower. Insects buzzed past their heads. Mountains, buttes, and bald knobs could be seen miles away. Gabe thought the scenery was like another world, compared to the high plains country where he'd been raised. The heat was powerful and almost palpable, as if it could be cut with a knife.

Gabe and Sally were sweating profusely, and so were the

horses who plodded onward across the endless desert. Gabe wondered how Apaches could live in such a hostile climate. He'd seen no game and wondered what they ate. He'd been told many edible plants grew on the desert, and the Apaches knew how to harvest them.

Gabe didn't see any more Apaches. Around noon, he decided to stop for lunch. He pulled his horse to a stop and stood in the stirrups to see where he was. He was surprised to notice in the distance a small stand of trees and other vegetation which indicated the presence of a water hole.

"What's wrong?" Sally asked.

"I see a water hole, I think."

He urged the dun onward, and Sally followed him on the apaloosa. The horses threaded their way through the cactus and finally came to the area where the trees and plants were. It was like entering another world, with the water hole in its center. Gabe dismounted and led his horse to the hole, where it bent its head low and drank. Sally led her horse to the hole and let it drink too. Then she lay on the ground and touched her lips to the cool sweet water.

She drank deeply of the water, while the horses slurped it up beside her. It was cooler in the shade of the trees, and she felt revived. Gabe stood to the rear of his dun, looking around suspiciously, his hand on his gun. If somebody wanted to pull an ambush, this was the ideal place to do it.

She finished drinking and stood. "Damn, that was good."

"Stand watch, while I take a drink."

She pulled out her gun and examined the vegetation nearby as Gabe kneeled beside the waterhole and scooped his hands in the water. He raised the sparkling liquid to his lips, and it went down like silk, just what he needed. Bending for more water, he heard a *twang* sound somewhere behind him, and a second later an arrow swooshed into the water next to him.

"Get down!" he shouted.

Sally dived to the ground. She'd seen the arrow streak through the air and was horrified. Gabe yanked out his pistol, dropped onto his belly, and scanned the trees in the direction that the arrow had come from. He couldn't see anything, but knew at least one Apache was out there.

"Are you all right?" he called out to Sally.

"Yes, are you?"

"Stay low to the ground. Fire at anything that moves."

Just then Gabe heard another twang. The arrow came down from a tree in front of him, and the arrow slammed into the ground a few inches from his face. Gabe fired three shots at the tree, and heard a scream. The tree shook, and an Apache fell out of it, a splash of blood on his chest.

Gabe looked around for cover, because he and Sally were in the open next to the water hole. "Follow me!" he shouted.

He jumped up and ran toward the trees. Sally came up off her stomach and followed him. Arrows flew through the air, and one of them pierced Sally's left sleeve, tearing the flesh on her forearm. It happened so fast that she didn't have time to scream. She and Gabe dived into the bushes next to a tree.

"You're hit!" he said.

She was in a mild state of shock. One moment she'd been drinking out of a water hole, and the next, Apaches were shooting arrows at her.

Gabe unbuttoned her cuff and rolled it back to reveal the wound. The cut didn't look too bad, but it was bleeding profusely. Gabe tore a handful of leaves from a tree and pressed it against the wound. An arrow rammed into the tree that they were hiding behind.

"Are you all right?" Gabe said to her.

"I think so."

"Bet you wish you would've stayed in Gleeson."

"What're we going to do?"

"They don't have guns, otherwise they would've used them. They're probably just a raiding party. Maybe they'll attack or maybe they'll go away. You'd better lie down."

"I'm not as weak as you think I am."

She raised her rifle and jacked the lever, looking around the tree, as blood continued to drip from her arm. Gabe couldn't help admiring her grit. She was no shrinking violet.

He held his rifle in his hands and hoped the Apaches would attack. But they probably wouldn't attack. They wouldn't run into the barrels of guns. They'd try to sneak up on their quarries and take them by surprise. Gabe wondered how many Apaches were out there. He guessed not many. Maybe they were the three he'd seen riding earlier in the morning. Those Apaches might have guessed correctly that he and Sally would stop at the water hole.

Gabe looked back toward the water hole. Their two horses had run away. He and Sally were stuck in the middle of the desert with a bunch of bloodthirsty Apaches, and there was no way out.

"I guess the folks in Gleeson were right," Gabe said. "This is no time to be on the desert."

"We'll get out of this somehow," she replied.

Gabe listened to the sounds of the desert, but all he could hear was a faint breeze passing through the foliage. Where were the Apaches? He looked at the wound on Sally's arm, and the blood was coagulating.

Suddenly he heard a blood-curdling scream. An Apache with a hatchet in his hand erupted out of a bush nearby and charged toward him. He didn't have time to fire a shot; the Apache was on top of him. The Apache swung down with his hatchet, and Gabe raised his rifle to block the blow. The handle of the hatchet slammed down on the stock of the rifle, and the Apache gritted his tobacco-stained teeth, reaching with his free hand toward Gabe's face, trying to gouge out his eyes.

There was a loud *whump* sound, and the Apache's eyes rolled into his head. He dropped to his knees, and Sally stood behind him, her rifle in her hands. She'd just slugged him over the head with her rifle butt.

Gabe aimed his rifle down and shot the Apache, who was no more than a teenager, like Sally. Perhaps this was his first war party.

Sally was pale. The events of the morning were becoming too much for her. She'd been wounded in the arm, and now, lying in front of her was a dead Apache. She'd never seen anybody get shot before. Her jaw hanging open, she sat on the ground at the base of a tree.

"How're you doing?" Gabe asked.

"I'll be all right," she said weakly.

Gabe wondered how many more Apaches were out there. Now he was sure they didn't have guns, because they would've used them by now. He heard the sound of another *twang,* and a second later an arrow was sticking out of his right bicep. Then the pain hit him. A shot rang out, and an Apache fell forward out of a bush.

"I got him!" Sally shouted.

The Apache lay still on the ground. There was silence around the water hole. Three Apaches were. dead, and that was the number Gabe had seen earlier on the desert. Was that all of them?

He thought it might be. His right arm felt as though it was on fire. He looked at it, and the arrow had gone all the way through his bicep. The pain was ferocious, but the Sioux had taught him how to withstand pain. Gritting his teeth, he pushed the arrow deeper into his arm, so the arrowhead would extend farther out the other end. Then he grasped the arrowhead with his free hand and snapped it off. He grabbed the feathers at the end of the shaft and pulled the arrow out of his arm.

Sally watched with grim fascination as he yanked out his knife and cut off a length of his pants.

"Tie this on for me," he said to her.

She tied the makeshift bandage around his wound. "Are you all right?" she asked.

"Yes."

He worked his right arm after she was finished. It hurt but evidently there was no serious damage because it moved fairly normally. The pain was intense, but that was the least of his problems.

"I think we got them all," Gabe said.

"How do you know?"

"I don't know. I'm just guessing there were only three. How're you holding up?"

"Don't worry about me," she said.

"I'm not worried about you. I just wanted to know how you are."

"I'm all right, I guess."

Gabe got to his feet and picked up his rifle. Fortunately he was left-handed and could use it without much serious difficulty.

If he were alone he'd reconnoiter the area and look for the Apaches' horses. They had to be somewhere around the water hole, but other Apaches might be about too. Maybe he hadn't killed all of them.

He couldn't bring Sally with him because she'd make too much noise. She'd have to stay behind and look out for herself.

"You sure you're okay?" he said to her.

"I told you I was."

"I'll have to leave you here alone for awhile."

"What!"

"I've got to take a look around. If anything moves near here, shoot it."

She opened her mouth to protest, but knew she shouldn't. She'd already promised not to be a burden to him. Besides, she had a six-gun and a rifle, and knew how to shoot. "Hurry back," she said.

He crawled away and was swallowed up by the thick foliage surrounding the water hole. She was alone. She glanced around nervously. An army of Apaches could be in the trees nearby, watching her hungrily, for all she knew. She was scared, but not so much that she couldn't think clearly. If any Apaches attacked her, she'd kill as many of them as she could before they got her.

Apaches had been in her mind all her life. She'd grown up in the Southwest and had heard stories of Apache atrocities almost from the time she could walk. It was a reality that all white people had to live with. Some of her cousins had been killed by Apaches during a raid on their ranch. She knew it was a harsh country, and had never expected anything else.

The desert became silent except for the chirping of birds and insects. Sally held her rifle tightly and examined her surroundings back and forth, up and down. She knew she had to stay vigilant if she wanted to stay alive.

She thought of how drastically her life had changed during the past twenty-four hours. Yesterday she'd been chafing under the restrictions of life at her parents' store, and today she was a free woman, out on the desert with a strange man who'd taken her virginity the previous night. She'd been dreaming for the past several months about becoming free, and now she was. It was a heady feeling, but scary too.

She wondered what Gabe thought of her. She imagined he figured she was just a silly little kid, and he probably regretted sleeping with her because now he was stuck with her. She swore she'd never be a burden to him or anybody else. She'd stand on her own two feet even if it killed her.

She dreaded the inevitable separation they'd have. He said he'd take her to the nearest town, and that'd be it. She didn't want to tell him so, but she was in love with him. He was so strong and good-looking, and he was kind too. He'd taken pity on her and let her travel with him.

She'd always wondered what it'd be like to sleep with a man, and now she knew. She'd sometimes suspected that it might be awful, but it wasn't awful at all. In fact, it had been terrific.

She looked down at the two dead Apaches near her feet, and was jolted back to reality. She'd been thinking about how Gabe made her tingle, but she might be dead within an hour. Perhaps an Apache was drawing a bead on her just then. She crouched low on the ground and held her rifle tightly, her finger curved around the trigger. The rifle was loaded and ready to fire. *Come on, you dirty Apaches,* she thought. *I'm not afraid of you.*

Meanwhile, Gabe crawled through the underbrush, pausing every several feet to listen and search for Apaches. He paused behind a boulder and looked up at the trees, but couldn't see anything. Slowly and laboriously, he roved around the water hole. Then he heard the snort of a horse.

He stopped and listened. Perhaps the Apaches had a guard with the horses. He heard a hoof striking the ground. Moving forward, he peered through the leaves and saw three bareback horses tethered to trees. There were three dead Apaches. It all totalled up. There were no more live Apaches at the water hole.

The horses were skitterish. Gabe knew that Apaches didn't treat horses so well. They rode them to exhaustion and then ate them. Gabe untied the horses and led them toward the water hole. "Sally!" he called out. "We got all the Apaches!"

She came out of her hiding place and met him at the water hole, where he let the Apache horses drink. One of the horses had a brand on it; evidently it had been stolen from a ranch.

"You stay here," Gabe told her. "I'll look for our horses."

He jumped onto the horse with the brand and rode it out of the vegetation surrounding the water hole. His horse and Sally's weren't far away; they were grazing together in a swale. He took their reins and led them back to the water hole, where he found Sally sitting on the fallen trunk of a tree, looking somber.

"Let's move out," he said.

They climbed onto their horses and rode west toward Tucson. Gabe wanted to put as much distance as possible between him and the water hole, because Apaches probably used it regularly.

The sun was at its peak in the sky, and Gabe wasn't accustomed to the heat. It made him feel dizzy as his horse trudged across the desert sand.

They rode along silently, rocking back and forth in their saddles. Occasionally they sipped water from their canteens.

Under the brim of his hat, Gabe's eyes continually darted left and right, looking for Apaches. They could be hiding anywhere, waiting to ambush him. He wanted to go slack in the saddle, but didn't dare. He had to pay attention if he wanted to survive.

Beside him, Sally thought she was going to faint. The sweltering heat was too much for her. She felt light-headed and weak, but didn't dare complain. Her nose and throat were dry as the desert sand. She didn't think she'd make it through the day.

Finally Gabe thought they'd put enough distance between them and the water hole. "Okay," he said. "Let's stop for a rest. Open some tins of beef for lunch."

They dismounted near the shade of a cottonwood tree. Gabe filled his hat with water and let each horse drink, while Melissa opened the tins of beef. They sat beneath the cottonwood tree and ate sandwiches made of biscuits and beef.

"How're you holding up?" he asked.

"Don't worry about me. How's your arm?"

"I can use it fairly well. Let's stay here for awhile, until the temperature goes down."

He lay back underneath the tree and closed his eyes, thinking they should travel at night when it was cool, and sleep during the day. The heat was like a furnace, and there was no escape. It was even hot beneath the cottonwood tree.

He rested for a few minutes, then sat up. It wouldn't do to relax his vigilance for too long. Sally sipped water from her canteen.

"That was just what I needed," she said.

"You're a helluva woman."

She looked at him and smiled. "I love you," she said simply.

Gabe didn't know how to reply. He always became nervous when women told him they loved him.

"Why don't you take a nap," he said to her. "I'll stand watch for you."

She lay on her back and covered her face with her hat. Gabe looked at her firm breasts standing up pertly. If there weren't the danger of Apaches, he'd be tempted to take off her clothes. Her long legs were especially inviting.

Gabe looked away from her. She was too much of a temptation, and he had to keep his eyes open. He knew that Indians were trained in stealth, and one of them could creep right next to you before you knew it, if you didn't pay attention.

He rolled a cigarette and lit it with a match. Tucson was around fifty miles away. They'd probably arrive in two or three days. Then he'd say goodbye to her.

But he didn't want to say goodbye to her. He wanted to stay with her for awhile. She was pretty, and had an inner strength that he admired. Gabe wondered what it'd be like to settle down with somebody like Sally. He wouldn't be able to roam around like a vagabond anymore, but maybe he'd like domestic life. He could buy a ranch and raise horses and cattle. Other men had done it, and so could he.

He thought it was a good idea. Sally was the kind of woman a man could rely upon. She'd stood her ground against the Apaches back at the water hole. Another woman might've become hysterical, but she'd been calm and steady throughout the ordeal, although she'd probably been scared to death. *I think I'm falling in love with her*, he said to himself.

In the hidden canyon, Cibicue the medicine man sat in his cave and poured handfuls of sand onto the floor. At his feet were piles of different colored sand, which would be incorporated into the sand painting he was making. Its subject was Apache warriors defeating blue coats in battle. He spread the sand with his long bony fingers and formed the crude pictures. There were four ranks of Apache warriors, because four was a magic number to Apaches, and the blue coats were running away from them. Many blue coats were dead, lying on the ground with arrows sticking out of them. Cibicue used small slivers of wood to represent the arrows.

The sand painting wasn't an original. Cibicue had learned it from an older medicine man, his predecessor, Running Deer. Sand paintings were passed from medicine man to medicine man with only minor modifications. Earlier examples of the particular sand painting might've substituted Mexican Cavalrymen or Comanche warriors for the blue coats.

A sand painting was made and destroyed between sunrise and sunset of the same day. Cibicue hoped to finish the painting soon. He'd destroy it that evening, as the sun was sinking on the horizon. Perhaps by then a great victory would be won over the blue coats.

The sound of a loud cheer came to his ears. Cibicue arose and stood at the mouth of his cave. Below him in the valley he saw a vast number of new warriors entering the hidden canyon. Cibicue narrowed his eyes and focused on their leader. He saw that it was Eagle Claw, an Apache chief almost as famous as Diablito. Cibicue was surprised to see Eagle Claw enter the hidden canyon. Evidently Eagle Claw had left his reservation, too, taking all of his warriors with him.

Not far away, in another cave, Diablito heard the cheering. He'd been sleeping late, because he'd stayed up most of the night praying to *Ussen* and receiving visions. He stood, adjusted his breech clout, and walked to the mouth of his cave. Below him, he saw the band of new warriors advancing across the floor of the canyon.

Like Cibicue, he was surprised to see the warriors. Then he heard someone climbing below him. He looked down and saw Spider Arms moving quickly toward his cave. "It is Eagle Claw!" Spider Arms shouted. "He is here!"

Diablito's heart swelled with joy. Eagle Claw was a cousin and close friend. Like Diablito, Eagle Claw had gone to a reservation after Gray Wolf had hunted him down. Now Eagle Claw had chosen freedom too.

Diablito tied his red bandana around his head and came out of his cave. He patted Spider Arms on the back and descended the mountain, joining his warriors who were walking forward to greet Eagle Claw.

Eagle Claw dismounted and walked toward Diablito. The two cousins smiled at each other and embraced warmly.

Eagle Claw spoke first: "When I heard you left your reservation, I decided to leave too," he said.

"My heart fills with happiness," Diablito said. "We will make war together against the blue coats."

Diablito added up the numbers in his mind. Together they would be able to field almost one hundred warriors, a formidable force in the desert. He placed his arm around Eagle Claw's shoulder. "Come, my cousin. Let us eat together and discuss our plans."

Gabe placed his hand on Sally's shoulder. "It's cooler now," he said. "We'd better get moving."

She opened her eyes and saw the bright blue sky overhead. For a moment she didn't know where she was, because she'd been sound asleep. Then she remembered it all. She was out on the desert with Gabe Conrad, and earlier in the day she'd shot an Apache.

She sat up on the desert sand and looked at Gabe, who was standing beside her, tightening his belt. "How long was I asleep?" she asked.

"About two hours."

"I'm so tired."

"We've got to push on."

She understood. They couldn't linger on the desert while Apaches were on the loose. Rubbing her eyes, she got to her knees, shook out her hair, and stood. He leaned toward her and kissed her lips.

"You're beautiful when you're asleep and you're beautiful when you're awake," he said.

"You were watching me?" she asked.

"Yes."

"You were supposed to be looking for Apaches."

"I did that too."

Each of them felt desire for the other, but they didn't have time. They had to press on toward Tucson. They loaded their supplies onto the pack horse and mounted up.

Gabe led the way west, and Sally followed at his side. She noticed that the sun wasn't as hot as it had been earlier in the day, but it was still quite warm. The two riders moved across the desert, and the only sound they heard was the hoofbeats of their horses.

Gabe sat in his saddle and rolled a cigarette. He lit it with a match and thought he and Sally should stay on the trail until sunset, when they could stop again for another quick meal. Then they'd ride all night and sleep tomorrow during the day in a safe hiding place. They'd also have to look for another water hole.

The sun beat down on them mercilessly, but not as intensely as earlier in the day. Soon the routine of riding took over again. The horses plodded onward and the two riders rocked in their saddles, searching around for signs of Apaches.

An hour passed without anything happening. Sally thought of her home back in Gleeson, and realized she didn't miss it at all. It had been like a prison. Freedom was enthralling, even if it was dangerous. But it wouldn't be dangerous once she got to Tucson. She'd be safe there, able to build a new life for herself.

She was a little worried, because she knew it wouldn't be easy to get a job in Tucson. Many unattached young women on the frontier became sporting ladies, or in other words, prostitutes. Sally didn't want that to happen to her, and the very thought of it made her shudder. But she could read and write and do numbers. Hopefully that would get her a good job.

About an hour later, Gabe held up his hand.

"What's wrong?" she asked.

"Look."

She looked straight ahead but didn't see anything except the desert. "What is it?"

"Somebody's been by here."

He dismounted, handed her the reins for his horse, and walked forward. Now she noticed that the desert sand ahead was churned up more than usual. Gabe advanced toward the tracks and kneeled down, examining them. The marks were of unshod horses, which meant they were ridden by Apaches. They were headed north and he estimated that the tracks were approximately eight hours old. He saw the marks of travois, which meant the Apaches were travelling with household gear, women and children. There had been nearly sixty horses. Had Diablito come this way?

He walked back to his horse and mounted, telling Sally what he'd seen.

She looked around, wondering where the Apaches had gone. "Do you think they're nearby?" she asked.

"If they were, we wouldn't be alive right now. Let's move out."

They prodded their horses and continued across the desert.

Eagle Claw wore the claw of his namesake on a leather thong around his neck. Nearly sixty years old, he still was sinewy and powerful. His face was deeply creased by his many years of exposure to the desert sun, but his hair was jet black, with no streaks of gray.

Tejan, Diablito's wife, brought them both cups of water from the sacred lake. The two chiefs drank deeply.

"It is good to be with you again, my cousin," Diablito said. "I never thought I would see you again."

"*Ussen* has brought us together to make war against the blue coats," Eagle Claw said. "That is the way I see it."

"That is the way I see it, too."

"It is all so sad," Eagle Claw said, and shook his head in despair. "I remember when I was a boy, and the desert was Apache land. Now the blue coats and the white eye settlers are squeezing our lives out. They show us no mercy. The Coyote has sent them to make us suffer."

Eagle Claw was referring to the Apache god of evil, Coyote, who caused all the misfortune and suffering in the world.

"Yes my cousin," Diablito said, "but now we are together and we have enough warriors to fight back. Our problem is that we need horses, guns, ammunition, and food. The white eyes have many small towns and ranches where we can get these things. Tomorrow we go in search of them."

"But the blue coats . . ." Eagle Claw said.

"We are many now," Diablito replied. "*Ussen* protects the

brave. The blue coats will furnish our weapons and ammunition. We will attack them when they are weak and we are strong. We must be smart like the fox and quick like the deer. We will leave the women and children here and spread death upon the land.''

"You speak wisely," Eagle Claw said. "It is good to be with you here in the hidden canyon. My soul gets sick when I think about the years on the reservation."

Diablito smiled. "Think instead of victory, my cousin. Soon it will be ours. We will be strong again, and then we will go south to Mexico."

"It will be as you say," Eagle Claw said.

Gabe stopped his horse and stood in the stirrups, holding his hand over his eyes and looking straight ahead. Sally reined back her horse too, but didn't see anything.

"What is it?" she asked, frightened.

He didn't reply, instead gazing ahead at the desert. Far off, he saw a cloud of dust that indicated the presence of riders moving in their direction. Whoever they were, their destination was probably the water hole that Gabe and Sally had left earlier in the day. Gabe looked around for cover. To his right was a thick range of chapparal.

"Over there," he said to Sally. "Hurry."

"What've you seen?"

"Somebody's coming, and I don't know who they are."

They wheeled their horses to the right and galloped toward the chapparal. Gabe hoped the riders weren't Apaches, and if they were Apaches, he hoped they hadn't seen them. He and Sally might be able to hold off a few Apaches, but not as many as were coming.

They rode behind the thick chapparal and dismounted. Both sipped water from their canteens. Gabe peered through the chapparal and saw the cloud of dust come closer. "Will you be all right here alone?" he asked her.

"Where are you going?"

"I want to see who they are."

"Take me with you."

"I can move faster alone, and make less noise."

She hated to be left alone, but she'd promised not to be a bother to him. "All right," she said. "I'll do what you say."

He pulled his rifle out of the boot and winked at her. "I'll be back in a little while, but if I don't come back, try to make it to Tucson on your own."

"I could never make it to Tucson on my own."

"It'll be your only chance, if the Apaches get me."

"Don't let them get you, Gabe."

"Keep your eyes peeled and your rifle loaded."

He bent low and crawled into the chapparal. In seconds, he was gone. She couldn't even hear him anymore. She was alone again, and an awful sense of solitude and danger came over her. She looked around, and recalled hearing stories of Apaches who could camouflage themselves so adroitly that you wouldn't know they were standing a few feet away.

Her eyes examined the dense chapparal. Apaches could be surrounding her, for all she knew. They could rip her apart with their knives or shoot her full of arrows.

She broke out into a cold sweat. Taking deep breaths, she sought to calm herself. If Apaches were around, Gabe would've noticed them. He'd been raised by Indians and knew all the tricks. He wouldn't lead her into a trap, would he?

She glanced around warily. Gritting her teeth, she planted her two feet firmly on the ground and aimed her rifle straight ahead. She was afraid, but not too afraid to fight. But she wished Gabe hadn't left her. She didn't want to be alone on the desert.

Then she heard something move in front of her, and nearly fainted with terror. Something was in the bushes! It moved again.

"Who's there?" she said.

There was no answer. Then she heard a grunt and a rustle of branches. She aimed her rifle at the sound. A dark form appeared near the ground. It pushed forward and poked its head into the tiny clearing. It was a wild pig with tusks jutting up out of its jaw. Sally took a step backwards. "Get away from me," she said.

The wild pig walked into the clearing and looked up at her. She pointed her gun down at him. If he made a wrong move, she'd blow him away. She'd heard that wild pigs could be ferocious when mad, but this one didn't look mean. In fact, he looked kind of friendly.

"What do you want?" she asked.

He sniffed, burped, and turned away from her, walking into the chapparal. She watched him go, and realized her heart was beating wildly. He'd scared her nearly to death!

She sat down, took off her hat, and wiped the fear-sweat from her brow.

Gabe crawled forward through the underbrush. He passed a tall saguaro cactus and then a cottonwood tree. He moved across the terrain swiftly and silently, on a path that would intersect with the oncoming riders. He peered through the bushes and saw the cloud of dust coming closer. It was headed straight for him now. All he had to do was wait.

He lay on the ground and pressed his ear against the sand. The earth transmitted the sounds of the horses' hooves, and it sounded as though the horses were shod. That meant they were U.S. Cavalry! But he couldn't be sure. He'd have to wait and see for himself.

He thought of Sally, and hoped she was all right back there. He'd hated to leave her alone, but couldn't take her with him whenever he went someplace. She hadn't been raised by Indians and didn't know how to move silently.

He could hear the riders now. It sounded as if they were carrying a lot of metallic equipment, which was more evidence that they were cavalrymen. But he didn't dare expose himself yet. They might be Apaches who'd killed cavalrymen and stolen their horses and equipment.

Gabe crept forward and looked ahead. The riders were visible now and he saw their blue shirts and yellow hats. They were white men, not Indians. Gabe heaved a sigh of thanks and stood up.

He walked in their direction, holding his rifle in his right hand. Moving into the open, he stood and waited for them. They still were pretty far off and probably couldn't see a man on foot yet, so he waved his rifle in the air to attract their attention.

He heard the troop commander shout an order, and the troop stopped. Then a lone rider advanced forward. He was a white man wearing a dirty tan shirt and a floppy brown hat. His beard was brown and hung down to his chest.

"Waal," the man said as he approached, "what in hell've we got here?"

"My name's Gabe Conrad, and I've got a woman with me."

"I'm Jack Scoones, scout for Troop C. What're you doin' in the middle of the desert?"

"I'm on my way to Tucson."

"What happened to your arm?"

"Ran into three Apaches at the water hole back there."

"Didn't you know the Apaches were on the loose?"

"I heard Diablito was off the reservation."

"He ain't the only one. Now Eagle Claw's off the reservation, too. That's a helluva lot of injuns. You must be crazy to be out here alone with a woman. Where the hell is she anyway?"

Gabe pointed his thumb behind him. "Back there."

"You're lucky you're still alive. I think you'd better join up with us."

"I think we should too. Let me get my horses and the woman."

"I'll report to Captain Donahue."

Scoones wheeled his horse and galloped back toward the main body of cavalry. Gabe ran back to where Sally was hiding.

"It's me!" he shouted. "Don't shoot!"

She waited for him in the clearing, holding her rifle ready just in case. "What is it?" she asked.

"U.S. Cavalry!"

She closed her eyes. "Thank God."

"We should be safe now," he told her. "Saddle up."

They climbed onto their horses and rode out of the clearing. Threading their way through the brush, they came to the main trail and waited for the advancing cavalry. Sally was so happy she wanted to shout. She'd been afraid of getting killed by Apaches, but now she was safe. She swore that she'd never go out onto the desert again in her life unless she was well-protected, or all the Apaches were on reservations.

The cavalry troop approached, hoofs thundering on the ground, jingling and jangling equipment. Troopers carried their guidons in front with the officers and scouts. Gabe recognized

Scoones among them. An officer raised his hand and the troop came to a stop in front of Gabe and Sally. A cloud of dust billowed forward and enveloped them all.

"Hello there," said an officer with a brown mustache. "I'm Captain Donahue, and this is Lieutenant Robbins." He indicated a young officer with blond hair. "Who might you be?"

"I'm Gabe Conrad, and this is Sally Barnes."

"What the hell you doing out here?"

"We're on our way to Tucson."

"Heard you ran into some Apaches."

"Yes, at the water hole back there. Killed three of them."

"This is no time to be on the desert. I think you'd better join up with us."

"I'm not arguing with you," Gabe said.

"Where you coming from?"

"East."

"That's where we're headed. We're looking for Diablito."

"Ran into some Indian sign back there," Gabe told him. "About sixty horses, I'd estimate, heading north. They had women and children with them."

Captain Donahue looked at Lieutenant Robbins and Jack Scoones. "Could be Eagle Claw," he said. Then he turned to Gabe and Sally. "Care to show us where you saw those tracks?"

"Sure."

"Let's ride."

Captain Donahue raised his hand in the air and moved it before him. "Forward hoooooo!" he hollared.

The troops advanced, guidons hanging slack in the hot, breezeless afternoon. Gabe maneuvered his horse to the left of Captain Donahue, and Sally rode beside Lieutenant Robbins, who tipped his hat gallantly to her, a gesture that Gabe noticed and didn't like.

The sweat of horses and men's bodies assailed Gabe's nostrils. He thought the troop of cavalry was making a terrific amount of noise. It felt strange to be travelling with soldiers, after spending so many days in the saddle alone.

"How's your arm?" asked Captain Donahue.

"Not too bad."

"Was it a bullet or an arrow?"

"Arrow. If they had rifles, the outcome might've been very different."

"They probably wanted *your* rifles."

"That's what I figured."

Captain Donahue turned sideways to Gabe. "Tell me, Mister Conrad—where'd you learn to read sign?"

"Oh, some fellers taught me a long time ago."

"You sound as if you can read it very well. What fellers taught you?"

Gabe hated to talk about it, but he saw no point in lying. "I was raised by the Sioux until I was fourteen," he explained. "They taught me."

"Raised by the Sioux? How come?"

"My mother was captured by the Sioux when she was pregnant with me."

Captain Donahue waited for more, but Gabe looked ahead and rode silently. Donahue realized Gabe wasn't going to say more, and he wasn't one to pry.

Lieutenant Robbins picked up on the conversation. "If you were raised by Indians," he said to Gabe, "you must be sympathetic to their cause."

"I am in a way."

"How do we know you're not a spy for Diablito?"

"Guess you don't know."

"Sir," Lieutenant Robbins said to Captain Donahue, "I suggest we keep this man under surveillance. He might be leading us into a trap."

"I'll take your suggestion under advisement," Captain Donahue said.

Lieutenant Robbins turned red with embarassment. Once more, Captain Donahue had failed to follow his sensible suggestions. The men were learning that Donahue didn't take him seriously, and that was bad for discipline.

Lieutenant Robbins had graduated from West Point only last year, and was eager to advance his career in the Army. He'd served briefly on Eastern posts, and then volunteered for the Arizona Command. His request had been approved, probably because his father was a Colonel in the War Department in Washington D.C.

Lieutenant Robbins turned and looked at Gabe, and didn't like what he saw. What was the man doing out on the desert when Apaches were on the loose? There was something wild and unsoldierly about Gabe that Robbins didn't like. And what was he doing with the woman?

Lieutenant Robbins looked at Sally, and thought she was quite pretty. He liked the way she sat tall in the saddle. What was she doing with Conrad? Somehow it all didn't add up.

"Where were you headed?" he asked Sally.

"Tucson," she replied.

"What were you going to do there?"

"Get a job."

"Doing what?"

"I don't know."

"Mister Conrad," Lieutenant Robbins said, "what were *you* going to do in Tucson."

"You ask too many questions," Gabe told him.

Somebody behind him guffawed, and Robbins turned even redder than he'd been before. The men were laughing at him. They thought he was a joke. At the Point, they'd never taught him how to deal with a situation like this. All he could do was press his lips together and be furious at Gabe. He decided to continue with his questions.

"Why won't you tell me what you were going to do in Tucson, Mister Conrad? Got something to hide?"

"It's none of your business what I was going to do."

"I think there's something fishy about your story."

"I don't care what you think."

Gabe knew he wasn't being very conciliatory, but didn't care. The U.S. Cavalry had attacked his village when he was a boy, and killed many of his friends. He didn't feel very friendly toward the cavalry, but he didn't feel friendly toward the Apaches either. They'd tried to kill him and Sally at the water hole earlier in the day.

Sally listened with amusement to the exchange between Gabe and Lieutenant Robbins. She couldn't understand why men constantly bickered and fought with each other. They were like bulls in a corral, always looking for trouble.

Troop C made its noisy way across the desert, and Sally felt safe. This caused her to relax her vigilance, and fatigue set in. She felt like going to sleep. The sun still was hot, pounding her into the saddle. She hoped they'd stop soon and make camp.

Captain Donahue sat firmly in his saddle, his eyes darting about as he looked for Apaches. He was a seasoned Indian fighter, the veteran of nearly twenty years in the Army. He'd served under Custer during the last two years of the Civil War, and had helped break Pickett's charge at Gettysburg. Since the war he'd been languishing in the Arizona Command. He had no friends or relatives in Washington, and fully expected to be a captain until he retired. His commission had been won on the battlefield, not at West Point. He didn't like Lieutenant Robbins very much.

"Where are those tracks you said you ran into?" Captain Donahue asked Gabe.

"About a mile ahead."

Donahue was an old war dog. He hated inactivity and loved the action of war. It made him feel alive, as opposed to garrison duty, which bored him to death. He thought that maybe he could make major if he could win a great victory against the Apaches. He wanted desperately to find Diablito and Eagle Claw, but not just for the sake of his career. Every man, woman and child on the frontier was in danger as long as those two savages were on the loose.

The cavalry troop tromped across the desert. Gabe looked back and saw the dusty sweaty soldiers riding with their neckerchiefs over their noses. They were getting the bulk of the dust. Gabe and the officers in front were breathing fresh air.

Gabe recognized familiar landmarks. He realized the Apache tracks were just ahead. "We're getting close," he said to Captain Donahue.

Robbins cleared his throat. "I think we should get ready for an ambush, sir," he said.

"We've got our flankers out," Donahue replied. "Tell the men to keep their eyes open."

Lieutenant Robbins turned to grizzled old Sergeant Callahan. "Tell the men to keep their eyes open."

*"Keep your eyes open, you sons-of-bitches!"*

Lieutenant Robbins gritted his teeth. He hated Sergeant

Callahan's constant profanity. "There's a lady present," he admonished Sergeant Callahan.

"Sorry, sir. I'll keep it in mind next time."

There was a note of mocking sarcasm in Sergeant Callahan's voice, and Lieutenant Robbins wanted to slap him across the face. Discipline in the troop was terrible, and he believed it was all Captain Donahue's fault. Captain Donahue should make the men drill more. Drill inbued men with the best traditions of discipline, or at least that's what they'd taught Lieutenant Robbins at West Point.

Gabe had listened silently to the conversations going on around him, and concluded there was much animosity in the cavalry troop. Lieutenant Robbins was a snotty brat and somebody had to take him down a peg. Gabe hoped he wouldn't have to remain with the troop very long.

He looked at Sally riding beside him. She looked as though she was drooping in the saddle. "You all right?" he asked her.

She straightened her backbone and raised her chin. "Don't worry about me. How's your arm?"

"It's not bad."

His arm still hurt, but he could move it around fairly well. It'd be able to hold a rifle steady should that become necessary. No serious damage had been done.

Gabe looked ahead and saw the spot where he'd crossed the Apache trail. "It's over there," he said to Captain Donahue.

Captain Donahue raised his hand, and the troop thundered to a halt behind him. He and Gabe dismounted, and walked ahead to where the Apache tracks were. Lieutenant Robbins, Sergeant Callahan, and Jack Scoones dismounted also and trudged behind them. Gabe came to the tracks left by the Apaches and pointed down.

"There they are."

Captain Donahue turned to Jack Scoones. "What do you make of them, Jack?"

Scoones dropped to his hands and knees and examined the tracks. He lifted some of the dirt in his hand and let it drop slowly to the ground. Then he stood, walked several paces, and dropped down on his hands and knees again. He smelled the ground, traced the outlines of hoofs with his finger, and then arose again, wandering from one side of the trail to the other. Finally he sauntered back to where Captain Donahue was.

"It's like Mister Conrad said," he explained. "About sixty-seventy warriors with women and children. Tracks are about eight hours old."

"Hmmm," said Captain Donahue, stroking the stubble on his jaw. "I wonder if it was Diablito or Eagle Claw."

"Can't say for sure, sir."

Meanwhile, Lieutenant Robbins glanced around nervously, his hand on his service revolver. He expected Apaches to attack at any moment. Sergeant Callahan giggled.

Lieutenant Robbins nearly turned green with rage. "What are you laughing at!" he screamed.

"Something caught in my throat, sir."

"I know you're laughing at me! Don't think you're fooling me!"

"Who, me, sir?"

"Yes, you!"

Captain Donahue looked at Robbins. "Relax," he told him.

"Sergeant Callahan's being insubordinate again!"

"I said relax."

Captain Donahue looked in the direction of the tracks. They were headed straight for a mountain range far in the distance. The mountain range was glowing red now that the sun was sinking toward the horizon. He wondered where the Apaches had gone. They probably had a hideout in those mountains straight ahead. In the old days, under General Crook, Apache scouts would've been used to lead the way to the hideouts, but now most of the good Apache scouts had left the reservation, and the ones remaining were no damned good.

Donahue added the numbers in his mind. He figured Diablito had about sixty braves, and Eagle Claw led approximately the same number. Had they joined forces? He had no way of knowing. His mission was to hunt down Apaches and destroy them, or bring them back to the reservation. He couldn't turn around and go away. His troop comprised fifty men and officers, well-armed with the latest weapons. The Apaches weren't so well armed. He decided to follow the trail and see where it went. He was an old wardog and he didn't run away from a fight.

"Let's mount up," he said. "We'll follow the trail."

Lieutenant Robbins stepped forward, his face blotched with emotion. "But sir, we may be riding into an encirclement."

"If we do, then we'll break out of it. Now mount up. I've just given you an order."

"What about the woman, sir?"

"We can't abandon our mission just because of a woman. Besides, she's probably safer with us than anywhere else. Now let's go, Lieutenant. I'm not going to tell you again."

They walked back to their horses. Gabe wondered if he was going from the frying pan into the fire. He'd been in danger when he was alone with Sally on the desert, but maybe it was worse being with the U.S. Cavalry. Captain Donahue evidently was looking for a fight. He, too, wondered if Diablito had joined up with Eagle Claw. Two tribes of screaming fanatical warriors would be hard to beat.

They climbed onto their horses. Captain Donahue pointed in the direction of the trail. "Forward hoooo!" he shouted.

High up in the mountains, an Apache warrior named Taza was on guard duty. He was short and barrel-chested, with thick legs and a wide mouth that turned down at the corners.

Like all Apaches, he'd been trained since childhood in improving his vision. Apaches stared at faraway objects for long periods of time, strengthening their eye muscles and powers of visual discrimination. An Apache could see farther and more clearly than a white man because of this intensive training.

Taza sat crosslegged on a ledge and stared at the horizon, his eyes roving back and forth. He wore a red bandana to hold his hair close to his head, and a red line had been painted across his cheeks and nose from ear to ear.

He had a rifle with him, a bow and arrow, a pistol, and a knife. He knew he and the other guards had the most important missions in the encampment, because the very safety of the encampment depended upon them.

He sipped some water from a container made from a cow's stomach, then scoured the horizon with his eyes again. He examined the terrain back and forward and up and down. He'd been in position for two hours and would be there two hours

more. All the warriors in the two bands alternated on guard
duty.

His head jerked barely perceptibly. Something was out there.
He squinted his eyes. There was movement on the horizon.
Clenching his jaw, he sharpened the focus of his eyes. It was too
far away to see distinctly, but it looked as if a large number of
riders was there, headed toward the mountain.

It could be more Apaches or it could be blue coats. Taza
would have to make sure. They were many miles away and
didn't present a danger yet, if they were blue coats.

Taza strained his eyes as he tried to focus more acutely. High
on the mountain, he could see a tremendous breadth of desert
beneath him. He waited patiently until the riders came closer,
and then he saw the blue of cavalry uniforms.

Electrified, he stood up and shook his rifle. The blue coats
were coming. He must tell Diablito immediately.

He scrambled down from the ledge and ran along the
mountain paths, his footing as sure as a cat's. The paths
criss-crossed each other as they descended the mountain, and
the Apaches in the valley watched his progress. He was moving
quickly and they knew he'd seen something. The warriors
climbed the side of the mountain to see for themselves.

Taza came to Diablito's cave. He stepped inside and waited
for his eyes to adjust to the dimness.

Diablito's voice came out to him. "What is it, Taza?"

"Bluecoats coming."

"How many?"

"Cannot see exactly how many, but a big number."

Diablito stepped out of the darkness. At his side was Eagle
Claw. They followed Taza out of the cave and climbed to the
ledge where Taza had seen the blue coats in the distance.

Taza pointed. "There."

Diablito looked. The bluecoats were close enough to count.
There were fifty or sixty of them, and Diablito smiled. His force
outnumbered them. Apaches never liked to attack unless they
had a good chance of winning, and Diablito thought he'd have
that chance now that Eagle Claw's band had joined up with him.

The blue coats would have many rifles and much ammunition.
They'd have food and other useful equipment like knives,

blankets and bridles. Perhaps their horses could be captured. Diablito smelled a great victory coming.

Something was happening down there. The blue coats appeared to be stopping. Diablito narrowed his eyes. Yes, it was so. They were stopping. The sun was dropping low on the horizon and the blue coats were making camp. A line of green near the blue coats indicated that a stream was there. The blue coats would sleep beside the stream.

Diablito turned to Eagle Claw and smiled. Eagle Claw smiled back. There was no need to talk. Each knew what the other was thinking. They would attack at dawn.

# CHAPTER THREE

"We'll camp here for the night," Captain Donahue said. He turned to Gabe. "I hope you and Miss Barnes will be able to join me for dinner."

"I don't see any other place to eat around here," Gabe replied with a smile.

"We'd be happy to have dinner with you," Sally said. She felt starved to death.

The cavalry troop dismounted. Sergeant Callahan ordered a detail to gather the horses and picket them alongside the stream. The rest of the men set to work establishing the camp. Gabe looked at the sun dropping toward the horizon in the west. The giant red orb gave the desert a reddish glow.

Captain Donahue sat heavily beside a bush and rolled a cigarette. He felt fatigue deep in his bones. *Just a few more years and I'll be able to retire,* he said to himself. *All I have to do is hang on a few more years.*

Gabe and Sally sat down next to him. "I don't want to tell you your job, sir, but I hope you post an adequate guard," Gabe said. "I had one run-in with Apaches today, and I don't want another one."

"Don't worry about the guard," Captain Donahue said. "It's already been taken care of."

A group of soldiers set up the big canvas command tent

nearby. Captain Donahue puffed his cigarette and watched the sun sink toward the horizon. Sally walked off into the bushes. Donahue turned to Gabe. "I hope you're not taking advantage of that little girl," he said sternly.

"I'm not taking advantage of her," Gabe said, "and she's not that little."

"No, she's certainly not little, but she's young. Where'd you meet her?"

"Why don't you ask her?"

"I'm asking you."

"I'd rather you asked her."

Captain Donahue frowned. Gabe rolled a cigarette of his own. Sally returned to where they were sitting and joined them.

"Where you from, Sally?" Captain Donahue asked.

"Not too far from here."

"Whereabouts?"

"Gleeson."

"I know Gleeson. How come you left?"

"I'd rather not talk about it."

"I hope you know what you're doing."

"I do," she told him firmly. "Don't worry about me."

Gabe felt proud of her answers. She was proving to be a toughie. He wondered if circumstances would permit him to sleep with her tonight. He'd certainly like to get his hands on her again.

Lieutenant Robbins approached and saluted. "The horses are picketed and the guard is posted, sir."

"Sit down and relax, Lieutenant."

Robbins sat down but he didn't relax. He looked at Gabe suspiciously. A bird flew past behind him and he spun around, reaching for his service revolver.

"You're awfully jumpy tonight," Captain Donahue said. "It's not good to be so jumpy. You're liable to shoot somebody by mistake."

Robbins blushed and yanked his hand away from his service revolver. He pulled out his pipe, filled it with tobacco, lit it with a match, and coughed violently. Sally burst out laughing. Robbins arose abruptly and walked away.

"A very strange young man," Donahue commented.

The soldiers built a campfire, and the sun dropped below the horizon. Night came to the desert while dinner was being prepared. Gabe took a walk with Sally. They touched shoulders and hips as they walked across the desert.

"I'd like to get away from those soldiers," Sally said. "I wish we could go to Tucson."

"Not with all the Apaches on the loose. We'd never make it."

She looked up at Gabe. "How long will we have to stay with the soldiers?"

"I don't know."

"What if the Apaches attack us?"

"We'll have to fight."

She shook her head. "I never knew, when I first set eyes on you, that so much would happen to me."

"You were a little too frisky for your own good," he said.

"I'm glad I'm free from my parents, but I don't know about the rest of it."

They were walking around the edge of the encampment, and beyond them was the vast sprawling desert. Stars twinkled in the sky and the moon perched on top of the mountains to the north.

"Tomorrow should be an exciting day," Gabe said.

"What makes you think so?"

"Just a hunch," he replied.

Not far away, Black Hawk crouched behind a cactus plant. His body was smeared with dirt and he wore twigs in his hair. If you looked straight at him you wouldn't know he was there.

He wasn't alone. Two other Apaches were also spying on the encampment from other vantage points. They were counting soldiers, weapons, horses, and reconnoitering the terrain. Diablito and Eagle Claw wanted to attack at dawn, and needed accurate information.

Black Hawk saw Gabe and Sally, and could have shot them with his bow and arrow, but it wasn't the time for killing. That would come tomorrow at dawn.

Black Hawk watched the couple, and his heart filled with

hatred. They symbolized the suffering, deprivation and humiliation he'd undergone at the reservation. White people used to
point their fingers and laugh at him. They treated him as if he
was a freak, when in fact he was a warrior.

Now the humiliation was over. Diablito had given Black
Hawk his manhood back. Better to die a warrior than live as a
buffoon.

The couple passed out of his line of vision. Black Hawk
waited several minutes, then moved forward to get a closer look
at the camp. His footsteps were silent; he glided along like the
breeze. Coming to a boulder, he paused and looked around it.
Directly ahead was the camp of the blue coats. He saw the
soldiers cleaning equipment and taking care of their horses. One
big tent had been pitched. Black Hawk counted the men. They
all had the latest rifles. Black Hawk wanted to creep forward and
steal one, because he desired a new rifle more than anything else
in the world. But he couldn't creep forward and steal one. He
might get caught, and that would alert the blue coats to the
presence of Apaches in the area.

Black Hawk was still as the rock. Only his eyes moved, as he
watched the blue coats' camp.

Gabe and Sally returned to the main camp. "Wait for me by
Captain Donahue's tent," he said. "I'll be right back."

"Where are you going?" she asked.

"I want to check on our horses."

"Why can't I go with you?"

"I didn't think you'd want to."

"Well I do."

They walked toward the stream, where the horses were
picketed, passing soldiers gathered around campfires. Some
sang old cavalry songs, others cooked pots of coffee. The air
smelled like woodsmoke and the desert had cooled to a
comfortable temperature.

The horses were a short distance away, tethered to the picket
line. A few soldiers were on guard duty, and among them was
wiry, sandy-haired Sergeant Clemm, who was smoking a
cigarette. He had a hip flask in his back pocket and had been
sipping from it.

"Waal," he said when he saw Gabe, "if it ain't the injun lover."

Gabe didn't bat an eyelash. He was accustomed to being insulted by people who didn't like Indians. Sergeant Clemm evidently had heard Gabe tell Captain Donahue that he'd been raised by the Sioux.

Clemm and the other soldiers gazed at Gabe with hostility in their eyes. They stood with their legs apart and their thumbs hooked in their belts.

"Let's get out of here," Sally said. "These men are looking for trouble."

"I'm not finished yet."

Gabe walked past the soldiers and checked the horses. He looked at their legs and ran his hands over their coats to make sure they'd been rubbed down. Bags of grain were nearby and he figured they'd been fed. Now they were resting. They'd need the rest, because tomorrow would be another hard day under the hot sun.

Gabe turned around, and Sergeant Clemm was standing in front of him, a crooked smile on his face. "What're you snoopin' around fer?" Sergeant Clemm asked.

"Just checking our horses."

"We don't like injun lovers around here."

"I can understand that," Gabe said, and he could. He realized that soldiers who fought Indians would have no great affection for them. Sergeant Clemm probably had friends who'd been killed by Indians.

"You stink like an injun," Sergeant Clemm said.

Gabe stiffened, and Sally saw him. She was standing a few feet away and knew that trouble was brewing. "C'mon Gabe," she said. "Let's have dinner."

"Be right with you."

Gabe moved toward her, but Sergeant Clemm got in his way. "Hidin' behind a lady's skirts?" he asked.

"What's your problem?" Gabe said.

"I don't like injun lovers."

"Get out of my way," Gabe said.

"Make me."

Gabe looked down at Sergeant Clemm. The man evidently

was looking for a fight. Perhaps he wanted to show his men how tough he was. Or maybe his hatred of Indians had warped his brain.

Sally tried to step between them. "Now gentlemen . . ." she said.

"Stay out of this," Gabe said to her, holding up his hand.

The tone of his voice was stern. She'd never heard him sound that way before, and she took a step backwards.

Gabe looked down at Sergeant Clemm. "I'm not going to tell you again," he said. "Either get out of my way, or I'm going right over you."

"I'd like to see you try it," Sergeant Clemm replied. He took off his campaign hat and threw it to one of his buddies.

Gabe figured it'd be an easy fight if his right arm hadn't been shot with an arrow that afternoon. He'd still be able to use that right arm, but it would be painful and weaker than normal. Otherwise, Gabe figured he and Clemm were nearly evenly matched. Sergeant Clemm was shorter than Gabe, but muscular and evil-looking. Both men stared at each other, and didn't flinch. Sally watched them, wondering what it was that drove men to fight. They were always at it, day and night, and what was it all for? Just foolish pride, from what she could see.

Gabe felt himself getting angry at Clemm. He was always running into stupid thick-headed sons-of-bitches who were looking for trouble. Sergeant Clemm was just another one of them. Gabe stepped forward and Clemm raised his fists. Gabe shot a sudden left hook to Sergeant Clemm's head, taking him by surprise. The blow connected, dazing Sergeant Clemm. Gabe pushed him out of the way and walked toward Sally.

Sergeant Clemm recovered his equilibrium and spun around, running and diving onto Gabe's back, clasping his arms around Gabe's neck. Gabe drove his right elbow back into the pit of Clemm's stomach, and Sergeant Clemm went *oof*, loosening his grip around Gabe's neck. Gabe grabbed Clemm's arms, bent down quickly, and threw him over his shoulder.

Sergeant Clemm tumbled through the air and hit the ground back first. The force of his landing knocked the wind out of him for a few moments. Gabe stood over him and looked down. "You want more."

Clemm was boiling mad. He was being humiliated in front of his men, and there was nothing worse than that. Growling like an animal, he got to his feet.

"C'mon Sarge," said one of his men, egging him on. "You can take him."

Sergeant Clemm raised his fists and moved them in circles as he crouched over and stalked Gabe. He hadn't shaved for several days and looked like some kind of weird animal. Then suddenly he charged forward, throwing his left fist at Gabe's face. Gabe dodged to the right and threw a left hook at Sergeant Clemm's gut. Gabe's fist buried itself into Clemm's stomach, and he doubled over in pain. Gabe delivered a sharp left uppercut to the tip of Clemm's chin, and he straightened up, bent backwards, and fell on his back again.

Gabe looked down at him. "Had enough?"

Sergeant Clemm gasped for breath. At one moment Gabe had been in front of him, and in the next moment he'd been gone. What the hell had happened? Whatever it was, it wouldn't happen again.

Sergeant Clemm climbed to his feet and raised his fists again. A group of soldiers from a campfire nearby heard the commotion and were joining the audience. Sergeant Clemm saw them coming and became aware of the necessity of defeating Gabe Conrad. The men wouldn't respect him anymore if he didn't.

The soldiers made a circle around the combatants, and cheered Sergeant Clemm on. The uproar attracted the attention of other soldiers, and they, too, left their campfires, running toward the picket line to see what all the commotion was about.

Gabe and Sergeant Clemm glowered at each other in the middle of the circle. Sergeant Clemm got low this time, so he'd make a smaller target, and charged again. Gabe feinted toward the right, and Sergeant Clemm veered in that direction, then Gabe darted to the left at the last moment and held out his foot.

Sergeant Clemm tripped over it and fell onto his face in the mud. A few of the soldiers laughed. Clemm raised his face and spit out dirt and stones. He was furious now, and jumped to his feet. Wiping his face with his hands, he planted his feet firmly on the ground and this time decided to wait and let Gabe come to him.

"No more fight left in you?" Gabe asked, a sarcastic smile on his face.

"Come a little closer, an' I'll show you how much fight I got left in me, you dirty injun lover," Sergeant Clemm replied.

Sally watched the fight in the midst of the soldiers, and was shocked by its brutality. But the spectacle was too fascinating for her to walk away.

Gabe knew he could pound Sergeant Clemm into the ground if his right arm was normal, but it wasn't. He'd have to continue the fight strategically, relying on maneuverability to make up for what was lacking in his injured right arm. He stepped forward as if he was going to attack Sergeant Clemm head-on, but at the last moment jumped backwards. Clemm swung at Gabe, but Gabe wasn't there anymore which left the sergeant off balance and wide open for a punch. Gabe didn't hesitate. He threw a straight left jab to Sergeant Clemm's nose, smashing flesh and cartilage, then hooked a left to the side of Sergeant Clemm's head. But Sergeant Clemm had a hard head. He shook off the blow and thundered a right into Gabe's belly, following with a left to Gabe's head.

Gabe felt mildly dazed, but not so much that he didn't know what he was doing. He stepped backwards, with Clemm charging after him. Gabe timed him coming in and walloped him in the mouth with his left fist. It was a powerful crunching blow, and Sergeant Clemm dropped to his knees.

"Had enough?" Gabe asked.

Sergeant Clemm dived forward and tackled Gabe around the waist. Both men fell to the ground, and Sergeant Clemm climbed on top of Gabe, raising his fist to punch him in the face. Sergeant Clemm threw the punch, and Gabe twisted to the side. Sergeant Clemm's fist pounded into the ground, and he broke something in his hand. He screamed, and Gabe pushed him off, then scrambled to his feet.

Sergeant Clemm stood unsteadily. He worked the fingers in his right hand and it hurt like hell. "You son of a bitch!" he hollered.

Sergeant Clemm charged and threw a volley of punches from all directions. Gabe stood his ground and blocked them all, looking for an opening, and when he found it, he shot his left fist straight through. The force of the blow knocked Clemm's head backwards. He covered his face with his hands, and Gabe hammered him twice in the gut. Sergeant Clemm lowered his arms to protect his gut, and Gabe went upstairs again, smacking him in the mouth and splitting his lip. Then Gabe brought his slow right arm around and whacked Clemm in the eye. It would've been a knockout punch if Gabe's right arm was normal, but the punch only dazed Clemm, adding to his stupified mental condition.

The world was spinning around Sergeant Clemm, and he knew he was losing the fight, but he wasn't the kind of man who gave up easy, and he fought best when he was hurt. Roaring like a bull, he ran at Gabe again, and Gabe waited for him to come close, blocked his first flurry of punches, snaked his leg in back of Sergeant Clemm, and pushed.

Clemm fell on his ass. He shook his head in amazement because he couldn't understand how he'd got there. He'd thought he was finally giving Gabe a beating, and then suddenly he was on the ground again. Frustrated, angry and humiliated, Sergeant Clemm rose to his feet yet again.

Clemm's confidence was badly shaken. His eye was swollen, his nose felt broken, and teeth were loose in his mouth. He looked at Gabe and saw that he'd inflicted no damage at all. He'd tried so hard and gained no advantage.

"Had enough?" Gabe asked.

Clemm charged again, punching as quickly and powerfully as he could. Gabe stepped backwards, ducking, parrying, and blocking blows. Finally Clemm's frustration got the best of him. He aimed a kick at Gabe's groin, and Gabe grabbed Clemm's leg in midair. Gabe pulled him off his feet and swung him round and round. Sergeant Clemm felt blood rushing to his head, and struggled to get free, but he was off balance and flying through the air like a bird.

Gabe swung Sergeant Clemm around, and then let him go. Clemm was launched into space. He kicked and struggled, waving his arms around in the air, and then landed head first in the stream.

The soldiers laughed. Sergeant Clemm's head bobbed to the surface. He blinked his eyes, wondering what had happened to him. The soldiers continued to laugh at him and he felt his face grow hot with shame.

"What's going on here?" asked a deep booming voice.

It was Captain Donahue. All the soldiers stared at him in horror for a few moments, then somebody shouted: "*Atten-hut!*"

The soldiers snapped to the attention. Even Sergeant Clemm stood at attention in the middle of the stream.

"What're you doing out there, Sergeant?"

Sergeant Clemm didn't know what to say. He sputtered and drooled, trembling with rage. Sally had to place her hand over her mouth to stop herself from laughing out loud.

"I just asked you a question, Sergeant Clemm."

"I don't know, sir."

"You don't know what you're doing in the middle of the stream?"

"No, sir."

"Were you taking a bath?"

"No, sir."

"Were you fishing, perhaps?"

"No, sir."

Captain Donahue could see that Sergeant Clemm's face was badly bruised. Evidently a fight had taken place. He looked around but couldn't find anyone else bruised. Who could Sergeant Clemm have been fighting with? Captain Donahue shrugged. The men were always fighting. It wasn't worth worrying about.

"Well, come on out of there, Sergeant Clemm!" Captain Donahue shouted. "You don't want to miss coffee, do you?"

On the far side of the stream, the Apaches had watched the fight with amazement. They were Black Hawk, Jamo, and He Who Walks Fast, and they wondered why the blond man with the long hair was fighting the blue coat. It was most strange to them.

They watched the blue coats walk away, leaving two guards behind. The three Apaches gazed greedily at the horses, because horses were like money to Apaches. The more horses an Apache had, the richer he was. A fortune in horses was across the stream, guarded only by two blue coats who weren't being very wary.

"Should we?" asked He Who Walks Fast.

"No," said Black Hawk. "That is not our reason for being here. Diablito will be angry with us if we do."

"Black Hawk is right," agreed Jamo. "We are not here to steal horses."

He Who Walks Fast gazed longingly at the horses. If he had five of them he could buy a young wife. His current wife was getting old and tired, and she made He Who Walks Fast feel old. He wanted someone young, so he could feel young again. But he knew Jamo and Black Hawk spoke the truth. They were there to spy on the blue coats.

"We have seen enough," said Black Hawk. "Let us return to the hidden canyon now."

Jamo and He Who Walks Fast nodded in agreement. They turned and moved back into the wilderness, heading for their horses picketed a half mile away.


Gabe and Sally sat near the campfire with Captain Donahue, Lieutenant Robbins and Jack Scoones. They were eating steak and beans from tin plates. Captain Donahue noticed Gabe's skinned knuckles. "So you're the one," he said.

"Beg your pardon, Captain?"

"You're the one who threw Sergeant Clemm in the stream."

Gabe didn't say anything. He sliced another morsel of his steak.

"Not talking?" Captain Donahue said.

"Yes, it was me," Gabe said.

Sally thought she should protect Gabe. "It wasn't his fault," she said. "Sergeant Clemm insulted him."

"What did Sergeant Clemm say?"

"I can't repeat it."

"I can," Gabe said. "He called me an Indian lover and forced me to fight him."

"How'd he force you to fight him?"

"He got in front of me and wouldn't let me pass."

Captain Donahue nodded. "I see."

Lieutenant Robbins chewed a mouthful of beans. "Fighting is

bad for discipline and morale," he said. "I think we should court-martial Sergeant Clemm. Unfortunately we can't do anything to Mister Conrad, because he's a civilian, but I think we should ask him to stay away from the men."

"How can I stay away from the men?" Gabe asked. "We're all here together in the middle of the desert."

"Don't talk to them. Leave them alone."

"Is that an order?" Gabe asked.

Captain Donahue interjected himself into the conversation. "No, it's not an order, because it doesn't make sense. We have to talk with each other out here." He looked at Gabe. "I thought maybe you could help Mister Scoones, since you've evidently done some tracking in your day."

"Anything you say, sir," Gabe said.

"May I add something, sir?" Lieutenant Robbins asked.

"What is it?" Captain Donahue replied.

"I'd like to protest respectfully, sir, the assignment of Mister Conrad as a scout. We don't know much about him, but we do know that he was raised by Indians. His allegiances still might be with them. How do we know he won't lead us into a trap?"

"I've made my decision," Captain Donahue said, "and you'll have to live with it."

"Yes, sir."

Robbins lowered his head and ate his food in sullen silence. He didn't like Captain Donahue and thought he was an oafish old fool.

Gabe turned to Captain Donahue. "I think we ought to expect action tomorrow," he said. "I know Indians, and I'm sure the Apaches have figured out exactly where we are right now, and where we're headed. I think they'll hit us when we least expect it, probably at dawn."

"We'll be ready for them," Captain Donahue said.

Sally was disturbed by the talk of a pending battle. "Do you really think there'll be fighting tomorrow?" she asked.

"Yes," Donahue replied. "I suggest you arm yourself, just in case."

"Sir," said Lieutenant Robbins, "don't you think we'd better turn back, since we have a woman civilian with us."

Donahue looked at him sternly. "We never break off a pursuit for any reason, Lieutenant. Those are our orders and we must follow them to the letter."

"I'm aware of the orders, sir, but I thought we should make an exception for the lady."

"We don't make any exceptions. This is war, Lieutenant Robbins." He turned to Sally. "Take cover quickly if there's any fighting," he said. "You're safer with us than you'd be if you'd stayed in Gleeson or were living on one of the ranches hereabouts."

"They're pretty scared in Gleeson," Gabe said.

"They've got good reason, but I don't think Diablito will attack them as long as we remain on his trail. That's why it's imperative that we stay after him like hounds after a rabbit. He'll be so busy with us that he won't have time to raid Gleeson or anywhere else."

"There's just one thing that bothers me," Gabe said. "If Diablito and Eagle Claw have joined forces, they probably outnumber us."

"But we have superior weaponry, Mister Conrad. I told you that before. Numbers alone aren't everything in a battle. Modern weapons make one trooper worth ten Apaches."

"I hope you're right," Gabe said.

"I think I am," Captain Donahue replied. "Colonel Sinclair at Fort Jerome feels the same way. That's why he sent out Troop C alone."

Lieutenant Robbins' hand trembled slightly as he continued to eat his steak and beans. He'd never been in combat before, and didn't know how he'd respond. Deep in his heart he was afraid that he might turn tail and run. Somehow he'd have to steel himself so he could stand his ground and fight like a man. He couldn't disgrace his father and his family.

Sally also was frightened. She'd never gone to West Point and wasn't trained to be a soldier. What if there was a battle tomorrow? What would she do?

Life had been so peaceful and simple before Gabe Conrad had ridden into her life.

• • •

The three Apaches signalled to the guard as they approached the entrance to the hidden canyon. The guard waved them on and they passed through the portals of stone, making their way to the lake, where they dismounted and picketed their horses. Then they climbed the cliff to Diablito's cave.

Diablito was sitting with Eagle Claw and Cibicue the Medicine Man, smoking cigaritos when the three scouts arrived. They greeted each other warmly and then the scouts sat on the floor of the cave.

Black Hawk made his report. He drew the configuration of the blue coat encampment on the ground, and showed its position relative to the stream.

"They have many horses," Black Hawk said, "and many rifles, with much ammunition. We saw one of the blue coats fighting with a white eye who was not a blue coat."

"I wonder what that means," Diablito said.

"Perhaps there is dissension among them," Cibicue the medicine man replied.

"There is always dissension among the white eyes," Diablito said.

Eagle Claw was looking at the map on the floor. "I think we should attack them at dawn from the four directions," he said. He pointed to the sides of the encampment where he'd like to strike.

"Why split our forces?" Diablito asked. "I think it would be better to strike them hard in one spot, and overwhelm them utterly."

"They might get away," Eagle Claw said. "We want to kill them all."

Diablito smiled thinly. "They will not get away."

Cibicue raised his finger in the air. "I think you're both wrong," he said. "The white eyes will expect an attack first thing in the morning. They will be ready."

Diablito nodded sagely. "That is true. They know that attacks come usually at dawn."

"I think you should attack them while they are on the march," Cibicue said. "We know the direction in which they are headed, and all we have to do is hide ourselves and wait for them. We should be still until they are near, and then strike from close range, where our arrows and lances will be most effective. The white eyes will not expect an attack when they're on the march, but if we attack in the morning, they will be waiting for us with their rifles."

Diablito wrinkled his brow as he thought about what Cibicue had explained. "What you say is true," he declared. He looked at Eagle Claw. "What do you think?"

"Cibicue has spoken wisely," Eagle Claw said. "I agree with what he has said. We must plan a clever ambush, one which the blue coats will not expect, and one from which they will not escape. We cannot permit ourselves to fail. Without rifles and ammunition, we cannot remain free for long. We need rifles and ammunition more than anything else right now."

"That is so," Diablito replied. "If we have rifles and ammunition, we can be free forever."

"We have decided on ambush?" Eagle Claw asked.

"We have decided," Diablito told him.

It was night in the cavalry encampment. Gabe lay on the ground, covered with his blanket and using his saddle as a pillow.

He rolled onto his side and gazed at the tent where Sally was sleeping. She was in there alone; the two officers had elected to sleep outside so she could have some privacy.

The encampment was quiet. Guards had been posted, but they were on the perimeter. Gabe wondered if he could sneak into the tent without being seen. He raised his head and looked around. Captain Donahue and Lieutenant Robbins were nearby. Jack Scoones and Sergeant Callahan weren't far away. What if one of them was awake?

It'd be embarassing if he were caught trying to enter Sally's tent. It might even create a serious incident. Soldiers could be unreasonable when their silly rules were broken. They believed in firing squads. Maybe it wasn't such a good idea after all.

But he couldn't stop thinking about Sally and her tall strong body, her delicious curves, her young firm breasts. She was so close, yet so far away.

Gabe thought it'd be especially bad for Sally if he were caught trying to sneak into her tent. The soldiers would consider her a tainted woman and treat her badly.

*No*, he thought, *I can't do it. I'll have to wait for some other time.*

He rolled over and tried to sleep, but couldn't stop thinking about Sally. He hadn't been too dazzled by her when he'd first met her, but now he realized what a special person she was.

He couldn't sleep; the tension was too great. He sat and rolled a cigarette, then lit it up. Looking north, he saw the mountain range, gloomy and ominous in the dim moonlight. *That's probably where the Apaches are hiding out.*

If he was an Apache just escaped from the reservation, the most important commodity for him after basic food and clothing would be rifles. The Apaches were doubtlessly hunting for rifles, and they wouldn't dare attack Fort Jerome. That meant they'd have to attack small units of soldiers, like the one he was with. Gabe was certain the Apaches would attack sooner or later. Dawn would be the most likely time. Captain Donahue had given orders that everybody would have to be awakened and ready for action two hours before dawn, just in case.

Gabe felt uneasy with the cavalry troop. They seemed to be blundering across the desert, hoping to find Diablito and Eagle Claw, but Diablito and Eagle Claw might find them first. Donahue seemed to be a well-intentioned officer, but he wasn't that smart. Robbins was inexperienced and impulsive, anxious to prove himself. Sergeant Callahan seemed to be a competent non-commissioned officer. Sergeant Clemm was a fighting fool. Jack Scoones was probably an able scout. The men in Troop C were the usual bunch of misfits and failures, but they'd fight well under pressure. Cavalry troopers usually could be relied upon to give a good account of themselves.

Gabe wondered how he'd got into the mess he was in. He hadn't realized he was riding into a war, but now that he was in one, he'd have to fight to survive. He'd heard about Apaches in his travels, and they were said to be the most ferocious fighters of them all, even worse than Commanches. Tomorrow he'd find out about them first hand. It would be a good day to die.

# CHAPTER FOUR

Gabe felt a hand on his shoulder, and opened his eyes. A soldier stood over him. "Time to get up," the soldier said.

The soldier walked toward Lieutenant Robbins. Gabe sat up. It was chilly and still dark on the desert. He saw Captain Donahue strapping on his saber. Gabe stood and stretched, then reached for his holster and tied it on. He pulled out his gun and rolled the cylinders, listening to the smooth clicks. Dropping his gun into its holster, he reached for his rifle.

He worked his wounded arm, and was pleased to notice that it was much better. It still hurt, and wasn't as strong as his good arm, but he'd be able to use it for nearly anything that might be required.

He looked around the encampment and saw soldiers carrying rifles sleepily toward the perimeter. From afar, he heard Sergeant Clemm shouting orders. Gabe saw Sally appear at the front of the command tent. Her blanket was wrapped around her shoulders. He walked toward her.

"Sleep well?" he asked.

"Not bad. How's your arm?"

"Much better. I wanted to pay you a little visit last night."

"Why didn't you?"

"I was afraid I'd get caught."

"Too bad."

They heard Sergeant Callahan's booming voice. "Everybody to the perimeter! Let's go, men!"

"I'll see you later," Gabe said to Sally.

Gabe carried his rifle to the perimeter of the encampment. He took a position behind a wagon and rolled his first cigarette of the day. The desert was silent and still, but a whole army of Apaches might be out there.

Gabe puffed his cigarette. Jack Scoones joined him. "See anythin' out there?" Scoones asked.

"No."

Scoones looked over the side of the wagon. "If they're out there, they won't attack us while we're ready. They'll attack us when we're not ready."

Gabe saw Captain Donahue and Lieutenant Robbins take positions not far away. The troop was ready for attack. If the Apaches came at dawn, they'd meet a withering hail of fire. Gabe found himself agreeing with Jack Scoones. The Apaches would never attack such a strong position.

The soldiers waited for the Apaches to attack. Dawn became a faint red glow on the horizon to the east. Some of the men had been detailed to brew coffee, which they poured into the soldiers' tin cups. One of them gave Gabe a tin cup, and he sipped coffee with the others. The men chewed on hard tack and waited for the Apaches.

The eastern horizon gave birth to the flaming orb of sun, and the desert was bathed in light. It became apparent to everyone that the Apaches weren't going to attack.

"Prepare to move out!" Captain Donahue shouted.

The soldiers pulled back from their positions. They hitched horses to the wagons and struck the main tent. Gabe dropped his saddle onto his horse and tightened the cinch straps. Then he did the same with Sally's horse. They climbed onto the horses and waited for the troop to form up.

Soldiers bustled around the encampment, gathering their equipment. Guards remained on duty just in case. The voices of Sergeants Callahan and Clemm could be heard issuing orders and bawling out slow troopers.

Finally, the men were ready to move out. They formed a long

double column in the desert with their horses and wagons. Gabe was in front with Sally and the officers.

"Forward hoooooo!" shouted Captain Donahue.

Troop C of the United States Cavalry advanced north across the desert, heading toward the mountain stronghold of the Apaches.

The cavalrymen didn't know it, but they were under observation. Diablito and Eagle Claw, along with several of their warriors and medicine men, sat on top of the mountain and watched the movement of the soldiers. Four Apaches scouts rode out of the hidden canyon to monitor the soldiers from close range. Diablito watched them go and murmured: *"Enjuh,"* which meant *it is good*.

In the valley, the warriors sharpened their knives and lances. They shot their bows and arrows at targets and cleaned the few old rifles that they had. In his cave, Cibicue made war medicine.

Phillip Jones, the white captive, watched the activity with dismay. He could see that the Apaches were going on the warpath. He wished he could be with his mother, but his mother was gathering mesquite with the Apache women.

Several of the Apache boys had invited Phillip to play with them, but he didn't want to. He hated the Apaches for killing his father and didn't want to have anything to do with them.

He wished he could escape and warn the settlers and ranchers that the Apaches were going on the warpath, but he couldn't escape. He didn't even know where he was.

The Apaches were friendly toward him, and he couldn't understand why. He despised them all. His mother, when he saw her, was always working. He'd spoken with her yesterday and she'd told him that she might have to become the wife of an Apache warrior.

Phillip was in a state of shock over what had happened to him. He wanted to do something, but didn't know what. All he could do was bow his head and cry.

Troop C made its way across the desert. The sun rose in the sky and the temperature climbed gradually. Flankers had been posted and Jack Scoones rode in advance of the column, looking for Apache sign. He didn't see anything, but that didn't mean Apaches weren't in the vicinity.

Four mounted Apache scouts stalked the column of cavalry, determining its direction and speed of movement. They tethered their horses and crept close to the column, watching as it passed, gazing greedily at the rifles the soldiers carried.

The soldiers were ready for ambush. Their rifles were loaded and ready to fire. They looked from side to side, ever vigilant, searching for Apaches. In the front of the column, Gabe felt that something was going to happen. He could smell it in the air. He wanted to advise Captain Donahue to return to Fort Jerome, but he knew Donahue wouldn't listen to him.

Captain Donahue had the tenacity of a bulldog. He was on the trail of Apaches and he'd maintain his direction until he could attack or they attacked him.

The Apache scouts watched their progress. They could see that the white eyes were following the trail left by the Apaches yesterday. That meant it would be easy to lay a trap for them.

The scouts returned to their horses and jumped on top of them. They galloped back to the hidden canyon and dismounted beside the sacred lake. Then they climbed the side of the mountain and reported to Diablito and Eagle Claw, who sat on a high ridge, watching the blue coats come closer.

Diablito listened to their report and grunted. They confirmed what he could see. The blue coats were being cautious, but not cautious enough. They were following a trail and therefore their direction could be predicted. It was time to go out and make war.

Diablito looked at Eagle Claw. They both understood what had to be done. Together they descended the side of the mountain. The warriors in the canyon saw them coming and gathered together their weapons. Their faces had been freshly painted and they were eager to kill the enemy.

The Apaches climbed onto their horses. Phillip Jones watched them. They looked fearsome and wild in their strange war paint. Phillip had never seen so many Apaches in his life.

Diablito and Eagle Claw rode to the entrance of the hidden

canyon, and the warriors followed them. The women and
children chanted a war song. Cibicue stood in front of his cave
and watched them pass. Then he raised his face to the heavens
and held out his arms.

"May *Ussen* grant them a great victory," he uttered.


At the front of the column, Gabe pulled the right rein of his
horse, to move in closer to Captain Donahue. "Sir," he said,
"May I make a suggestion?"

"What's your mind, Conrad?"

"With all due respect, sir, I think we should get off this trail
we're following. You're making it easy for the Apaches to
ambush us."

Donahue smiled indulgently. "That's the whole point. We
want them to attack. Our purpose is to fight them."

"But you don't want to fight them on their terms."

"We'll fight them on any terms. We're ready for them."

"They might be ready for us."

"We have the weaponry, Conrad. Don't forget that. They
won't be able to stand up to us. I appreciate your concern,
though. Thank you for your suggestion."

Captain Donahue turned away from him. Gabe veered his
horse toward Sally, who'd been watching him.

"What did you say to him?" she asked.

"I told him to get off this trail, but he wouldn't listen to me."

"What's wrong with this trail."

"He's making it easy for the Apaches to ambush us."

"Do you really think they will?" she asked, a note of fear in
her voice.

"Yes, I think they will. I hope I'm wrong, but if there's any
trouble, just stay close to me. Just remember that Indians
usually don't kill white women. They like to capture them and
make them slaves."

Sally grimaced. "My God."

"It shouldn't be too bad," he continued. "You'll just have to
chop wood and build fires, cook food and skin animals for
leather. You'll have to make clothes and gather food, picking
berries and such. Occasionally you'll have to make love to a

warrior, but that might be fun. Indians have wonderful ceremonies, dancing all night long. You might like the life. I certainly did.''

"I don't think I will," Sally said.

"You never know," Gabe told her.

Two eyes were staring at Gabe's back. The eyes were swollen and discolored, and belonged to Sergeant Clemm, whose heart was brimming with hatred.

Gabe had humiliated him last night, and Sergeant Clemm couldn't forget it. His men had been treating him with contempt all morning, and one even had talked back to him.

Clemm was tempted to draw his gun and shoot Gabe in the back. The consequences would be grim, but he thought it'd be worth it. Sergeant Clemm's teeth were loose in his mouth and he had a terrible headache. He desperately wanted revenge.

But he wasn't so desperate that he couldn't think straight. There was a way to kill Gabe so that he wouldn't get caught, and that would be if the Apaches attacked. During the melee, Sergeant Clemm could shoot Gabe, and everybody would think an Apache did it. That was the way to get rid of the bastard.

Sergeant Clemm found himself hoping that the Apaches would attack that day.

Several miles in advance of the cavalry troop, Diablito and his warriors rode south on the trail they'd made yesterday. Diablito knew he was on a collision course with the cavalry. They were straight ahead across the burning desert sands.

Diablito knew the terrain well. He'd roamed the Sonoran desert all his life. Ahead was a series of shallow rolling hills, an ideal spot for an ambush. That was where he and Eagle Claw had decided to strike at the blue coats.

The morning was hot, but it didn't bother Diablito. Apaches had incredible powers of endurance and were practically impervious to extremes of heat and cold. The band of warriors came to the shallow rolling hills and Diablito turned to Eagle Claw. Both of them pointed toward the left, and the band veered off the trail, riding into the chapparal. They continued for about a half-mile, then dismounted behind a hill, out of sight of the trail.

The horses were left in the care of younger warriors, and the main body of men trudged with their weapons back to the rolling hills. They dug holes in the ground and covered themselves with dirt and twigs. Then they lay in the holes and scooped dirt and vegetation over themselves.

When finished, the desert looked as pristine as it had been before they'd arrived. No one would ever guess that a hundred Apaches were lurking there, ready to attack.

The column of cavalry soldiers continued its advance across the desert. The sun rose in the sky and sent its flaming rays down upon them. Sweat soaked the shirts of the cavalry soldiers and the heat made them dizzy. They were sorry they'd ever joined the cavalry.

Most were from the East and never had been on a horse before they'd joined up. They'd seen recruiting posters that promised a life of adventure and excitement, but instead they'd got the hot dusty desert and a harsh life with low pay and lousy food.

They knew they could be attacked at any moment, but moments passed and they weren't attacked. That caused them to relax their vigilance. Their horses plodded over the trail left by the Apaches on the previous day. The heat caused the sand to shimmer around them. Sweat dripped down their foreheads and burned their eyes. Some had stomach aches. Others had headaches. They dreamed of cool water and naked women.

At the front of the column, Gabe was feeling increasingly uneasy. Something was wrong, he could feel it in his bones. His many years with the Oglala Sioux had given him a strange sixth sense. He could smell trouble.

He wanted to ride ahead with Jack Scoones and scout the terrain, but didn't think he should leave Sally. Somehow he felt responsible for her. If it hadn't been for him, she'd still be in Gleeson, sweeping the floor of her father's general store.

He looked at her. She was seated squarely on her saddle, her cowboy hat low over her eyes. He wanted to lean close and kiss her cheek. Weak, namby-pamby women had never interested him much. He liked the type who could put up a good fight.

He recalled how she'd fought hard at the water hole when they'd held off the Apache raiders yesterday. She hadn't whimpered once, but instead had fired her rifle as fast as she could.

She turned to him. "What's wrong?"

"Nothing."

"Why are you looking at me?"

"No particular reason."

She shrugged and faced front again.

*She's a tough one,* Gabe thought. *Maybe too tough for her own good.*

Diablito lay motionless in his hole, with a thin covering of dirt over him. He could hear the approach of the blue coats, and his heart beat faster. Beside him lay his rifle, his lance, his bow and arrow, and his knife. He was prepared to leap out of his hole and fight like a maniac.

He knew the importance of victory. With it, his warriors would remain a viable fighting force. Without it they'd be at a desperate disadvantage in future encounters with the white eyes, if they were still alive after today.

Diablito knew that his men looked to him for leadership. He'd have to set the right example and fight more savagely than anybody else. A warrior became an Apache chief principally on the basis of his fighting ability. His warriors followed him out of respect, not because of any laws.

Diablito had maintained that respect for nearly fifteen years, even during the sad time of captivity on the reservation. He'd led his people to freedom and now he must lead them to victory.

Everything depended upon the element of surprise. The blue coats must be attacked and overwhelmed quickly. Diablito pressed his ear against the ground. The blue coats were drawing closer.

Then Diablito heard a dissonant sound. One horseman was evidently riding in advance of the main body. This would be a scout trained to seek out Apaches. He would come to the region of rolling hills first, and might spot them.

Diablito considered his strategic situation. His warriors had departed from the main trail well in advance of the spot where they were going to spring the ambush. They were well camouflaged and ready to attack. The scout should see nothing.

Diablito closed his eyes. The scout was coming closer. He would soon be in the rolling hills.

Jack Scoones rode a chestnut gelding that was bigger and taller than most horses in the cavalry troop. He wore a floppy old leather hat, and his black and gray beard extended down to his chest.

He was fifty-two years old, but was still muscular and strong. His eyes weren't perfect, however. They'd worsened gradually over the years and he didn't know how bad they were.

Ahead, he saw the rolling hills, but they'd passed other rolling hills that morning and nothing had happened. Jack Scoones leaned forward in his saddle and scoured the countryside with his eyes, but saw nothing unusual. The Apache trail continued straight ahead toward the northern mountains.

Jack Scoones had been living on the frontier for most of his life. He'd been just about everywhere from the Black Hills in the north, to California in the west, and Texas in the south, but had settled in Arizona about ten years ago, working as a trader, hunter and scout.

He knew the Apaches well, and even spoke some of their language. He'd fought against them, made peace with them, and even had got drunk with them on occasion. He thought Apaches were fine warriors, and respected them for their fighting skill, but also thought they were thieving, superstitious savages who'd rather lie than tell the truth. Apaches made him suspicious. He liked some of them, but didn't trust any of them.

Riding through the rolling hills, he wondered when Troop C would make contact with Apaches from Diablito's tribe.

He didn't know it, but they were all around him at that moment.

Diablito heard the scout ride past him, only a few feet away. He didn't dare look up and see who it was, because he didn't want to give his position away.

He knew that the scout was probably somebody he knew, because he'd known most of the scouts from Fort Jerome. In fact, he'd been somewhat friendly with Jack Scoones, who was only a few feet away.

Diablito heard the cavalry advance toward him. It was only twenty or thirty yards away now. Soon the attack would begin. *Ussen,* he thought, *please grant us the victory that we need so much right now.*

Gabe saw the rolling hills straight ahead, and it looked like the perfect spot for an Indian ambush. He leaned forward in his saddle to see better, but nothing unusual came into his field of vision. He'd seen Jack Scoones ride into the area. It must be all right if he hadn't seen anything. Flankers were out, and they hadn't spotted Apaches either. Gabe thought maybe he was worried about nothing.

But the danger signal was buzzing in his mind. Something eerie was telling him that trouble was ahead. He knew that Captain Donahue might think he was crazy, but he thought he'd better warn him.

He prodded his horse, and it galloped to Captain Donahue's side. "Sir," he said, "I think we'd better take special precautions in that hilly area up ahead."

"We stay ready for all contingencies," Captain Donahue said.

"I suggest you order the men to hold their weapons ready."

"Their weapons *are* ready."

*Well, I tried,* Gabe thought. He eased his horse to the side and rejoined Sally.

"Hold your rifle ready to shoot," he told her.

"What for?" she asked.

"I think we're going to have trouble up ahead."

"What makes you think so?"

"I don't know."

Sally looked ahead and didn't see anything threatening. But she'd been with Gabe long enough to know that his instincts were generally good. There was no harm in being safe. She pulled her rifle from its boot and jacked the lever. Gabe drew his gun from its holster. Side by side they moved forward into the rolling hills.

Diablito heard the blue coats coming. His heart pumped wildly and blood rushed through his veins like electricity. He held his rifle tightly in his hands and prepared to jump out of his hole.

He had to be patient and wait until the entire troop was in the midst of the Apache ambush. That was the only way to achieve victory. He grit his teeth and felt the ground tremble as the blue coats rode past. They were only inches away. He opened an eye and could see their guidons fluttering in the breeze.

Only a few more moments. He kept his eye open and angled his head slightly. He saw the blue coats pass in two columns. In front were their officers and a woman with orange hair. Who was she? he wondered. The Apaches occasionally had woman warriors, but he'd never heard of a white woman who was a warrior.

Diablito felt an odd chill run up his spine. Was the white woman an evil omen? What was she doing with the blue coats? Perhaps she was a witch. Could the blue coats be using witchcraft against the Apaches? Apaches were very superstitious people. They believed in the power of witchcraft.

The soldiers rode past, making considerable noise with all their equipment. Diablito knew his warriors were tense as he, waiting for his signal to attack.

The time had come. The main body of blue coats was in the midst of the Apaches. To wait longer would permit the blue coats in front to get away.

Diablito leapt wildly out of his hole and screamed at the top of his lungs. He aimed his rifle at the nearest blue coat and fired. The rifle kicked in his arms, and the blue coat fell off his horse. Diablito didn't have time to reload. He dropped his rifle, ran forward with his lance, and hurled it through the breast of another blue coat.

All around him, Apache warriors swarmed out of their holes and attacked the blue coats, who were taken by surprise. They were shot, speared, and hacked, but some managed to dismount and fire their pistols.

Gabe's horse raised his forelegs high in the air at the first shout of Diablito. Gabe watched in amazement as the ground around him suddenly opened up and a horde of Apaches issued forth. His gun was in his hand and he opened fire immediately. His first shot downed an Apache rushing toward him with a lance. His second shot hit an Apache aiming a rifle at him. Then, from out of nowhere, something crashed into him.

It was an Apache warrior diving through the air, and the impact knocked Gabe from his horse. He fell to the ground, Apaches screaming all around him and one Apache on top of him, holding a hatchet poised in the air, about to crash it down on Gabe's skull.

Gabe raised his left hand and caught the Apache's wrist in midair. The Apache punched Gabe in the mouth with his free hand, but Gabe had always been able to take a good punch. He raised his midsection and tried to buck the Apache off him, as the Apache tried to punch him again. Gabe caught the Apache's fist in his right hand, and they rolled over on the sand. Gabe's back hit a cactus plant, and the needles stuck into his flesh, but he had more important things to worry about. The Apache struggled to break his hands loose from Gabe's iron grip, but Gabe was too strong for him. The Apache tried to knee Gabe in the groin, but Gabe twisted to the side and received the blow on his outer thigh. Again they rolled around on the ground, the sounds of battle ringing wild and loud all around them.

Gabe suddenly let go of the Apache, and jumped to his feet. He looked around for his gun but couldn't see it. The Apache lunged toward him again, swinging the hatchet at Gabe's head. Gabe timed him coming in and snatched the hatchet out of his hand. The Apache looked at his empty hand, amazed by the sudden turn of events. All he could do was pull out his knife, which bore a twelve-inch blade.

Gabe and the Apache circled each other on the frantic bloody battlefield. The Apache feinted but he didn't fake Gabe out. He feinted again, and Gabe swung the hatchet down. The blade buried itself in the Indian's shoulder, and the Apache howled in pain. Gabe drew the blade out and smashed the Apache in the face. The Apache crumpled to the ground and lay still.

Gabe didn't have time to exult in his victory. Soldiers and Apaches were grappling all around him. He jumped over the body of the fallen Apache and landed in front of another Apache who'd just run a soldier through with his lance.

The Apache yanked the lance out of his adversary and turned

to face Gabe. Gabe took a step back, measuring the Apache, and the Apache let out a war cry, pushing the lance forward toward Gabe's chest.

Gabe swung the hatchet to the side and broke the lance in half. Then, on the backswing, he caught the Apache on the side of the head. The Apache went down. Gabe stepped over his body and found himself facing an Apache who was aiming a cavalry pistol at him. Gabe dived to the ground just as the pistol fired. The bullet whistled over his head, and he leapt to his feet, charging the Apache.

The Apache couldn't cock the pistol again quickly enough. Gabe was on top of him, swinging down with the hatchet. The Apache raised his hands to protect himself, and caught the handle of the hatchet in midair, but Gabe kneed the Apache in the groin. The Apache's eyes rolled into his head and he screeched in pain. He dropped to his knees, and Gabe swung the hatchet sideways, lopping off the top of the Apache's head.

The Apache was hurled to the ground in a spray of blood. Gabe looked up and saw another Apache standing over Captain Donahue, who was lying on the ground, his cavalry sabre in his hand. The Apache held a lance in his hands, and was about to ram it through Captain Donahue's chest.

Gabe hurled the hatchet at the Apache, and it buried itself in his lungs. The Apache's knees wobbled and he fell to the ground. Gabe rushed toward the side of Captain Donahue, who lay on his back, his eyes half-closed and his breast covered with blood.

"I'm a goner," Captain Donahue said, closing his eyes.

Gabe heard an Apache war cry. He looked up and saw an Apache running toward him, a long knife in his hand. Gabe picked up Captain Donahue's cavalry saber and swung it with all his strength. The blade caught the Apache on the forearm and neatly severed it. The Apache stared with horror at his bleeding stump of an arm, and Gabe whacked him again with the cavalry saber, smashing in several of the warrior's ribs.

The Apache fell down and Gabe jumped over him. Standing directly in front of him was an Apache aiming a rifle at him. The Apache pulled the trigger before Gabe could move, and Gabe felt the heat of the bullet as it grazed his cheek. Gabe charged forward, and the Apache turned the rifle around, to use it as a club. He swung it at Gabe when Gabe came within range, and Gabe leaned backwards. The rifle butt narrowly missed his nose, and Gabe lashed out with the saber, catching the Apache on the neck, nearly chopping off his head.

The force of the blow threw the Apache on his side. Gabe pulled the saber loose and looked around. He saw an Apache perched on one knee, aiming a rifle at a cavalry soldier. Gabe ran toward the Apache and swung down the saber, striking the barrel of the rifle and deflecting its aim. The rifle fired into the dirt, and Gabe raised the saber again, then swung down swiftly, severing the Apache's spine. The Apache shrieked and fell on his face.

Gabe stepped over him. Two Apaches ran toward him, their lances aimed at his chest. Gabe looked around and saw a pistol lying on the ground nearby. He scooped it up and opened fire. The first bullet hit one Apache, and down he went, but Gabe couldn't cock the pistol in time to shoot the next Apache, who was right on top of him. Gabe threw the pistol into the Apache's face, and the Apache ducked. Gabe whacked the lance out of the way and grabbed the Apache by the throat, squeezing with all his strength.

Gabe's face and the Apache's face were only inches apart, and Gabe could smell the Apache's fetid breath. The Apache was a middle-aged warrior with a red headband and a red line painted across his nose and cheeks from ear to ear. The Apache struggled to break loose, but Gabe wouldn't let go. The Apache turned purple. His eyes bugged out of his head and his mouth gasped for air. Then he suddenly went limp in Gabe's hand. Gabe let him fall to the ground.

Gabe heard screams and grunts all around him as Apaches and cavalry soldiers killed each other. The battlefield was covered with dust, and it was hard to know who was winning. Gabe was barehanded and looked around on the ground for a weapon. All he could see was the lance belonging to the Apache he'd just choked to death.

He picked up the lance, and it felt comfortable in his hands, because it was similar to the lances the Oglala Sioux had taught him to use.

Gabe saw an Apache kneeling over a fallen cavalry soldier, about to crown him with a hatchet. Gabe let out an Oglala war cry and ran toward the Apache. The Apache, his hatchet poised in the air, turned in the direction of the sound, and was horrified to see Gabe thrusting the lance toward his chest.

The Apache jumped to his feet, but wasn't fast enough. The lance buried itself in his stomach. Gabe pulled the lance out and turned around. Another Apache with a lance was running toward him. The Apache pushed the lance forward, and Gabe parried it, bringing the butt of his own lance around and smashing the Apache in the face.

The Apache was dazed by the blow and his legs became rubbery. Gabe took a step backwards and slashed down with the lance, ripping into the Apache's shoulder and continuing diagonally down his chest, laying open flesh to the bone. The Apache bellowed horribly, and Gabe drew back the lance, then thrust it forward, burying it in the Apache's heart.

The Apache dropped to the ground like a lead weight. Gabe pulled the lance out of him and looked up. An Apache with a hatchet in one hand and a knife in the other hand ran toward him, screaming a war cry. Gabe planted one foot behind him for leverage and leaned forward, to stick the lance into the Apache's breast.

The Apache swung the hatchet at the lance, and deflected Gabe's aim, then brought the knife up toward Gabe's belly. Gabe jumped backwards and the blade of the knife sliced through the air. Gabe aimed the lance at the Apache again, and the Apache narrowed one eye, trying to figure out how to get past the lance. He decided that the best thing to do was charge and battle his way past it.

The Apache dug his heels in the ground and launched himself forward. Gabe feinted with the lance, and the Apache swung at it with his hatchet, but Gabe drew back the lance at the last moment. The Apache couldn't break his swing, and felt a sickening feeling in his heart, because he knew he was off balance and wide open.

Gabe thrust the lance forward with all his strength, and six inches of it plunged into the Apache's rib cage. Gabe tried to pull the lance out, but it was stuck in the Apache's ribs. He tried again to work it loose, but it wouldn't come out.

He heard an Apache scream behind him. Turning around, he saw an Apache flying through the air, a knife with its blade up in his fist. Gabe grabbed the Apache's wrist, spun around, and hurled the Apache over his shoulder. The Apache tumbled through the air and landed on his back, but he bounced like a rubber ball and was on his feet again immediately.

The Apache set his mouth in a grim line and advanced cautiously toward Gabe. Gabe had no weapon and saw none on the ground. He thought about running but didn't want to expose his back to the Apache, when suddenly the Apache leapt forward, thrusting the blade of the knife toward Gabe's belly.

Gabe grabbed the Apache's wrist in one hand and punched the Apache hard in the mouth with his other hand. The Apache was dazed by the blow, and Gabe kicked him in the groin. The Apache moaned as he dropped to his knees. Gabe kicked him in the face and knocked him cold. The Apache fell on his back and Gabe took the knife out of his hands.

Gabe looked up. Another Apache was standing in front of him, aiming an Army rifle at him, pulling the trigger. It was point blank range. Gabe didn't have time to get out of the way. Then suddenly the Apache staggered. He closed his eyes and fell to the ground. Someone had shot him.

Gabe couldn't see who'd shot him. The battleground was so dusty and confused it was hard to tell who was who. Shots rang out, men hollered, horses stampeded. Gabe looked around on the ground for a rifle or a pistol to fight with.

He didn't know it, but his life had been saved by Sergeant Callahan. The crusty old trooper, service revolver in each hand, was shooting his way across the battlefield. His shirt was torn and he'd been shot through the leg, but that hadn't stopped him. He'd lost his campaign hat and he had a cut on his forehead, the result of a glancing blow from a knife.

Sergeant Callahan peered through the dust and madness of the battle, and whenever he saw an Apache he shot him down in cold blood with either the pistol in his right hand, the one in his left hand, or both at the same time.

Sergeant Callahan didn't have to look for the Apaches. They kept coming to him, seeing the stripes on his arm and knowing he was a great blue coat warrior. Each Apache wanted the honor of killing Sergeant Callahan but none had done it yet.

Out of the swirling dust of the battlefield came another Apache warrior, carrying a lance. He let out a battle cry and charged Sergeant Callahan, and the stout old Sergeant took aim with the revolver in his right hand, pulling the trigger and bringing the Apache down.

Another Apache appeared, this one carrying a hatchet, and the brave sergeant turned toward him, took aim, and shot a hole in his chest. Sergeant Callahan heard something behind him and turned around. It was an Apache with an Army rifle, drawing a bead on him. Sergeant Callahan brought his pistols around, but the Apache fired first. Sergeant Callahan felt the bullet slice through his left shoulder, then he fired the pistol in his right hand, hitting the Apache in the stomach. The Apache dropped his rifle and bent over, hugging his stomach with his arms, and Callahan fired again, shooting the Apache through the top of the head.

Sergeant Callahan's left arm was numb, and he couldn't fire the pistol in his left hand anymore. His fingers didn't work properly and he couldn't maintain his grip on the pistol; it fell to the ground, but he still had the one in his right hand.

Three Apaches ran toward him, lances in their hands. Sergeant Callahan took cool, deliberate aim, fired one shot, and stopped one of the Apaches. He fired a second shot, and the next Apache bit the dust. Then he aimed at the third Apache, who was almost on top of him. Callahan squeezed the trigger, and the pistol went *click*. The chambers were empty. Callahan knew he was in deep trouble.

The Apache warrior thrust his lance forward, and it streaked toward Sergeant Callahan's chest. Sergeant Callahan deflected the lance with his left arm, and smashed the Apache in the face with his pistol. The force of the blow knocked the warrior cold, and he dropped to the ground at Callahan's feet.

Sergeant Callahan felt dizzy from loss of blood. He shook his head and tried to will himself back to clear consciousness. Reaching toward his ammunition pouch, he took out a fistful of bullets. Then he knelt on the battlefield and tried to load his pistol. It wasn't easy because his left hand refused to follow orders and hold the pistol still.

He didn't know it, but two eyes were watching him. They belonged to Taza, the short Apache with the barrel chest, thick legs, and wide, downturned mouth. Taza saw the big yellow stripes on the blue coat's arms and knew he was a great warrior. It would be an honor to kill such a warrior. Taza had captured a cavalry rifle, and aimed at the blue coat trying desperately to load his pistol. Something told Sergeant Callahan to look up at the last moment. He saw the Apache on one knee, aiming the rifle at him.

Sergeant Callahan tried to climb to his feet, but he was slow, he'd lost too much blood. Taza fired his rifle. Sergeant Callahan was knocked over onto his side. The bullet pierced one of his lungs and took away his remaining shreds of consciousness.

Taza jumped into the air and let loose a victory cry. Then he rushed forward to strip off the cavalryman's shirt, so he could wear it himself as a trophy. Taza knelt beside the old cavalryman and could see he was dying.

"You were a great warrior," Taza said. "Now all your power belongs to me."

He rolled Sergeant Callahan onto his back and saw that the shirt was covered with blood, but that didn't bother Taza. His squaw could wash the shirt and mend it after the battle was over. Taza unbuttoned the shirt and couldn't wait to put it on. He thought he would look splendid in it, and everyone would know he was a great warrior.

Taza heard a gunshot nearby, and it was the last thing he ever heard. He fell to the ground, a bullet hole in his head.

He'd been shot by Private Emilio Brouvelli, who had noticed the Apache warrior trying to steal Callahan's shirt. This was Private Brouvelli's first battle engagement, and he was torn and bloody but still standing.

A recent immigrant from Naples, he could barely speak

English. Short and skinny, with a long jaw and big ears, he'd been in America only three months. He'd worked in an ice factory in New York City, and the work had been boring. One day he'd seen a recruiting poster for the U.S. Cavalry, and he thought *what the hell, why not?*

Now he knew why not. He'd been slashed, shot, and bludgeoned, but somehow he still was standing. Turning around, he saw an Apache running toward him, a hatchet in his hand. Private Brouvelli fired his rifle from the waist, and the rifle bucked like a live thing in his hands. The bullet spun out of the bore and struck the Apache in the throat.

The Apache fell down, but Brouvelli heard another war cry. He looked to his left and saw another Apache grappling with Sergeant Clemm. The Apache's back was to him, and Private Brouvelli took quick aim with his rifle. He squeezed the trigger the way they'd taught him in training, and the impact of the bullet knocked the Apache over onto Sergeant Clemm.

Sergeant Clemm didn't know what happened, but the Apache was on top of him and he had to fight free. He pushed the Apache and was surprised at how easily the Indian fell off him. Then he realized the Apache was dead. He had no idea how the Apache had died, but he wasn't going to worry about it.

Wearily, Clemm got to his feet and looked around. The dust was so thick that he couldn't see more than ten feet in front of him. He looked around on the ground for something to fight with, and all he could find was the big knife in the Apache's hand.

Sergeant Clemm bent over and picked up the knife. Then he saw something move in the corner of his eye. It was a tall Apache wearing something strange around his neck. The Apache was aiming an Army rifle at him, and Clemm bounded to his feet.

"You thievin' son of a bitch Apache!" he shouted.

He charged toward the warrior, his knife in hand, and the Apache pulled the rifle's trigger. The rifle fired, and Sergeant Clemm felt a firestorm in his chest. Sergeant Clemm threw his arms out, dropped the knife, and fell onto his face.

Eagle Claw smiled. He'd been roaming the battlefield,

shooting blue coats, and now he'd just got another. It was so
easy when you had a good rifle.

He turned around, but the dust was thick. He couldn't see
anybody. But he could hear the sounds of blue coats and
Apaches cursing each other and trying to kill each other.

He wondered how the battle was going. He'd thought the
Apaches should've won by now, but evidently they hadn't won.
He heard a commotion to his left and ran in that direction,
looking for more blue coats to shoot.

Through the dust and smoke he saw a young white woman
with orange hair lying on the ground, aiming a rifle at him.
Eagle Claw was surprised to see her there, never having seen a
white woman fight with soldiers before. He paused for a
moment, and the woman fired her rifle.

Black curtains descended on Eagle Claw, and he fell to the
ground. Sally saw him fall, and he wasn't the only one she'd
killed that day. When the attack began, she'd jumped from her
horse and began shooting, and she'd been shooting ever since.
She'd been so busy she hadn't had time to think about what she
was doing.

An Apache nearby noticed Eagle Claw fall. He was Tona, a
member of Eagle Claw's tribe, and he saw that Eagle Claw had
been killed by a young woman with orange hair.

Ordinarily Tona would've tried to kill the person who'd killed
his chief, but he was spooked by the woman with orange hair,
who was aiming her rifle at him. She pulled the trigger, and
Tona felt as if a buffalo had run into his stomach.

He dropped to his knees and covered the bleeding hole with
his hands. "Eagle Claw is dead!" he gasped. "A witch with
orange hair has killed him!"

Black Hawk was nearby, and he ran toward Tona's voice.
Dust swirled around him and he saw Tona fall forward onto his
face. Then he noticed Eagle Claw lying on his back, a bullet
hole in his forehead. A bullet whistled past his ear, and he
dropped to the ground.

He saw the young woman with orange hair, wearing a white
shirt, and looking as if she'd come from another world.

"A white witch with orange hair has killed Eagle Claw!"
Black Hawk shouted at the top of his lungs, backing away from

the witch. "A white witch with orange hair has killed Eagle Claw!"

His loud voice carried across the battlefield, and Apaches everywhere heard what he'd said. They stopped whatever they were doing and felt stark terror. Ordinary people didn't scare them, but the supernatural drove them wild.

Diablito heard what Black Hawk had said, and he remembered seeing the white witch with orange hair when the battle had begun. The blue coats had powerful medicine, he now realized, and the Apaches would not be able to conquer them on this day, but there would be other days.

"Take all the rifles and ammunition you can, and back to the horses!" he yelled.

The Apache warriors disengaged from fighting wherever they were, and retreated east toward where their horses were tethered. The cavalrymen didn't try to stop them; they were glad to see them go. Some cavalry soldiers fired parting shots at Apache warriors and brought them down, but most of the remaining Apaches escaped from the battleground unscathed.

Gabe watched them go, holding a cavalry service revolver in his left hand and an Apache hatchet in his right hand. He had no idea of why the Indians were retreating. The battlefield became quiet except for the moans of the wounded and dying.

Gradually the dust cleared. Soldiers wandered around in a daze. The sand was covered with the blood and bodies of Apaches and soldiers. Cavalry horses could be seen milling around in the distance. Gabe wiped his forehead with the back of his arm. He had cuts and bruises all over his body.

The battle was over, but that didn't mean the Apaches would never come back. The Apaches hadn't surrendered; they'd just run away for some inexplicable reason. Gabe knew enough about Indians to realize something had spooked them, but didn't know what.

The Apaches hadn't been defeated. It had been Gabe's impression that they'd outnumbered the cavalrymen and were going to win the fight. Yet they'd run away, but Gabe doubted that they'd stay away. They'd pull themselves together and strike again. They weren't subdued yet by any means.

There was no telling when they'd attack again. The cavalry

soldiers had to reorganize quickly and figure out what to do. But who was in charge? Was Captain Donahue still alive?

Then he remembered Sally, and wondered where she was. A wave of anxiety passed over him. Was she all right?

"Sally!" he shouted. "Where are you?"

# CHAPTER FIVE

"I'm over here!" Sally hollered.

Gabe ran in the direction of her voice, passing cavalry soldiers wandering around in confusion, waiting for someone to tell them what to do. The end of the battle had come suddenly, for no good reason that they knew of. They were trying to make sense of what had happened.

Gabe jumped over Eagle Claw's body but didn't realize he was a chief. He saw Sally straight ahead, lying on the ground, a rifle in her hands. Around her were several dead Apaches.

"Are you all right?" Gabe asked.

"I think so."

"Can you get up?"

Slowly she rose to her feet, and Gabe looked her over. Her face was flushed with emotion, but otherwise she didn't have a scratch on her. He patted her on the ass. "You look like you're all right."

"You don't."

"Nothing's wrong with me."

Sally looked at the blood and gore on the hatchet in Gabe's hand, and felt nauseous. Lieutenant Robbins walked toward them, his service revolver in one hand and cavalry saber in the other. He was hatless and his uniform was torn, but he'd come through his baptism of fire and was happy that he hadn't broken and run.

An Apache had come at him with a hatchet as soon as the ambush began, and Lieutenant Robbins blew him away with his service revolver before he'd even thought about it. Still mounted, he'd shot more Apaches swarming toward him, and felt, for the first time in his life, the horror and eerie thrill of battle.

It was what he'd prepared for all his life, and he was ready for it. He'd emptied his pistol, climbed down from his horse, and fought Apaches hand to hand with his saber, remembering all the skills and special tricks he'd learned as a member of the West Point Fencing Team.

His saber had broken in half against an Apache hatchet, and he'd fought the Apache with his bare hands. He'd felt stronger than he'd ever been in his life.

He'd yanked the hatchet from the Apache's hand, killed him with it, and proceeded to waylay more Apaches. He couldn't say it was fun, because it had been scary as hell, but there had been something wonderfully stimulating about it.

Now, almost miraculously, the doubts he'd had about himself were gone, and he felt like a new man, as if his old self had died and he'd been reborn anew in the heat of battle. He had a new confidence and maturity, and walked with a certain swagger. At last he was a real soldier. He'd given a good account of himself on the battlefield and was proud. All the doubts he'd had about himself were gone. Hand-to-hand combat had made him a man.

"Miss Barnes," he said, "I'm glad to see you're all right. I was worried about you."

Sally didn't know what to say. She smiled thinly, trying to make sense out of what had happened. Yesterday she'd been sweeping her father's general store. Today she'd shot eight Apaches. She wondered if it was all a bad dream.

"I saw Captain Donahue out there," Gabe said to him. "He's dead."

Lieutenant Robbins nodded grimly. "Sergeant Callahan is dead too." He cupped his hands around his mouth. "Sergeant Clemm! Front and center!"

A voice came to him from across the battlefield. "He's dead."

"Corporal Debow!"

"Yes, sir!" replied a high-pitched voice from somewhere in the dust and smoke.

"Front and center!"

A heavyset potbellied trooper with brown hair ran toward them and saluted. A large swatch of shirt had been torn from his body, and he had cuts and nicks on his arms and face.

"You're the acting first sergeant from now on," Lieutenant Robbins said to him. "Have all the men assemble in front of me for a head count."

"Yes, sir."

Corporal Debow executed a smart about-face, stood at attention, and balled up his fists. "Troop—fall in!" he shouted in his strange tenor voice.

Soldiers assembled from all over the battlefield and formed ranks in front of him. Others limped slowly, bloody and battered, but still able to move. Gabe counted them. They numbered twenty-one men. More than two-thirds of the cavalry troop had been killed in the sudden encounter with the Apaches.

"Sergeant Debow," Lieutenant Robbins said. "Detail six men to gather together the wounded. The rest of the men will try to capture our horses. Any questions?"

"No, sir."

"Do it."

Debow turned around and shouted the necessary orders. The men dispersed on their separate duties. Gabe saw cavalry horses not far away. The battle had frightened them but not so much that they'd left the area completely. The troopers moved toward the horses, calling to them soothingly.

Lieutenant Robbins took his map out of his map pouch and spread it out on the desert sand. Then he sat cross-legged behind it and wondered what to do. This was the first time he'd ever commanded men in a combat situation. He tried to remember what they'd taught him at the Point, but somehow nothing seemed to fit his situation in the Arizona desert.

When Captain Donahue hadn't known what to do, he asked for advice from his sergeants and junior officers, but Lieutenant Robbins didn't have any sergeants and junior officers. All he had was Acting Sergeant Debow, who'd never seemed very bright.

"Sergeant Debow!" he shouted.

"Yes, sir."

"Get over here!"

Debow ran toward him and saluted.

"Take a look at this map, Sergeant."

Debow got down on his knees and squinted at the map. He appeared as if he didn't know what he was looking at. Gabe gazed down at the map over Lieutenant Robbins' shoulder. Sally hugged herself and wished she had some water, but all the water was with the horses.

Lieutenant Robbins pointed at the map. "We're here, and Fort Jerome is there. I think we should break off our patrol and head for Fort Jerome immediately. What do you think?"

Debow scratched his big round head. "I dunno, sir. Sounds all right to me."

Lieutenant Robbins was disappointed. He'd hoped to get some good advice, but instead had got servility.

"Supervise the horse detail," Lieutenant Robbins said.

Acting Sergeant Debow walked away. His theory of dealing with the cavalry was don't volunteer for anything and don't make any remarks that might be held against you later. Lieutenant Robbins looked at Gabe, who was standing beside him, still gazing down at the map. Gabe was cut and bloodied like the rest of them. Lieutenant Robbins realized it was ridiculous to have thought him an Indian spy. The man had said he'd been raised by Indians; possibly he might have some good ideas on how to proceed.

"What do you think, Conrad?"

Gabe kneeled beside Lieutenant Robbins. "I don't think you should head for Fort Jerome, because you might not make it."

"Why not?"

"Because you don't have many troopers left, and you'll be even more vulnerable than we were when we were just ambushed.

"What do you propose we do?"

"I think you should get together all your rifles and ammunition, your wounded, your horses and your supplies, and set up a defensive position in the hills over there. The Apaches will have an awfully hard time getting at you, compared to being out in the open on horseback."

Lieutenant Robbins scowled. "That's no good. We can't hold out forever here in the middle of the desert."

"You'll have to send someone to Fort Jerome for help."

"You mean send somebody all alone across Apache-infested country to Fort Jerome? What if he doesn't get through?"

"It's your only chance," Gabe said.

"No, I think it's better for all of us to go together."

"You'll never make it," Gabe said.

"Why not?"

"Because you just had a whole troop nearly wiped out. What'll you do with only twenty-one men? I don't know why the Apaches ran away, but if they didn't run away, we'd probably all be dead right now. They outnumbered us by at least two to one."

Lieutenant Robbins pondered that. He'd noticed during the fight that the troopers had been outnumbered by Apaches, and it was only a matter of time before the Apaches would swamp them.

"I wonder why the Apaches ran away," Lieutenant Robbins said.

"They thought we had stronger medicine than they did."

"What's that supposed to mean?"

"It's hard to explain to a white man."

"That's right, I forgot you were raised by Indians. Well, to go back to what you were saying before, about sending a courier to Fort Jerome, who do you think I should send?"

"I don't know," Gabe said. "That's your problem."

The Apache cohort rode through the portals of the hidden canyon, and the women and children came out of their caves to greet them.

The women and children were dismayed by what they saw. Many of the warriors were missing. No horses had been stolen. Most of the warriors were bloody and battered. Then they saw the dead body of Eagle Claw head down over a horse, and a terrible wail went up.

Diablito climbed down from his horse. He was cut and bruised, but at least he had a new Army rifle and almost two hundred rounds of ammunition. His heart was heavy. Many brave warriors had fallen in the fight, and the bravest of them all, Eagle Claw, had been killed.

Diablito and the other warriors led their horses to the stream and turned them over to the women. Then the warriors climbed the side of the cliff and entered their respective caves.

Diablito sat cross-legged on the floor of his cave. He knew, when he'd first set eyes on the witch with orange hair, that they'd have trouble. And they did have trouble. The blue coats had put up a stiffer fight than expected. Eagle Claw had been killed. No horses had been stolen. It hadn't been a defeat for the Apaches, but it hadn't been a victory either.

Diablito was troubled. The blue coats would be searching for him more diligently than ever. Fortunately he and his men had new rifles now. His band and Eagle Claw's had dropped to sixty-five warriors from over a hundred.

Who was the witch with orange hair and what was her strange power? He'd never heard of her before, but she must have powerful medicine if she was able to kill Eagle Claw. There was only one thing to do. Diablito would have to summon Cibicue the medicine man. Cibicue also had powerful medicine. Somehow he would have to counteract the medicine of the witch with orange hair.

Diablito thought of the fearsome witch as he'd seen her on her horse, riding at the head of the blue coat columns. A chill went up his spine, and he realized he'd made a terrible mistake. He should not have attacked the blue coats when they had the witch with orange hair to protect them with her medicine. Diablito was lucky that he hadn't been killed with Eagle Claw.

Diablito arose and walked to the front of his cave. He placed his hands around his mouth and called for Cibicue the medicine man.

Sally sat in the midst of the hills and drank water from an Army canteen. She was in a mild state of shock. Now that the fighting was over, she realized what she'd done. She'd shot and killed eight Apaches, and she'd never killed anyone else in her life.

She'd never thought much about death before. Occasionally

someone would die in Gleeson, and she knew she'd die someday, but she'd never worried much about it.

Now she was horrified by what she'd done. She'd shot Apaches and seen the agony on their faces as they'd fallen to the ground. One moment they'd been alive, and the next moment they'd been dead. It had all been so sudden and cruel.

She realized that life was a fragile thing. One bullet in the wrong place could end a life. She realized she'd been in serious danger during the battle. One stray bullet could've killed her easily; bullets had been flying all over the battlefield.

Lieutenant Robbins sat down next to her and held up a metal flask. "Look what I've got," he said, holding it up in the air. "It's whisky. Maybe you should take a drink."

Sally accepted the canteen. She didn't know how she looked, but she felt a little piqued. She unscrewed the cap and took a swig. The whisky rolled smoothly over her tongue and burned all the way down her throat. She coughed, and tears came to her eyes. Lieutenant Robbins patted her on the back.

"Take it easy," he said. "Here, have some water."

He passed her the canteen that she'd been drinking from. She swallowed some water and it soothed her throat. The whisky had made tears come to her eyes. She wiped the tears away and realized that she felt a bit steadier.

Sally looked around. The soldiers had devised a strong defensive position among the rolling hills. They'd pulled their wagons in and turned them over for protection. They'd gathered rifles and ammunition. Their horses were picketed nearby. Riflemen were posted in a three hundred and sixty degree circle. If the Apaches attacked, they'd face a formidable entrenched position.

A detail of soldiers was burying the dead. The wounded were lying on the ground near the horses. There were only five of them.

Gabe walked toward Sally and Lieutenant Robbins, carrying an Army rifle and an Apache hatchet. He had an Army revolver encased in his holster, and another jammed into his belt. He'd picked up a cavalry campaign hat and placed it on his head to protect himself from the bright sun.

He sat down next to Sally. "How're you feeling?" he asked.

"Lieutenant Robbins gave me some whisky to drink, and I'm much better."

Gabe scowled. He hated whisky because he believed it had destroyed many Indians. He thought it was bad medicine, and was tempted to lecture Sally on its evils, but decided to leave her alone. She'd been through enough that day.

"I've got a problem," Lieutenant Robbins said. "I don't know who to send to Fort Jerome."

"Send Debow. He seems to know what he's about."

"I'll need him here to help out in case the Apaches attack again. There's only one man here who could make it to Fort Jerome, and that's you."

"Uh uh," Gabe said. "I'm a civilian. Leave me out of this."

"You said you were raised by the Indians, and that means you probably could make the run better than anybody else here."

"One of your troopers should be able to do it."

"Most of them are green recruits, and the few veterans I've got left will be needed for the defense here. I still say you're the best man for the job. After all, you were raised by Indians. You know how they think."

"Not all Indians are alike," Gabe said. "I don't know how Apaches think."

"You must have some idea. Indians aren't that much different."

"Oh, yes they are."

Lieutenant Robbins threw up his hands. "I'm not going to argue Indians with you. Obviously you're the expert in that department. But we need somebody to go to Fort Jerome for help, and the way I see it, you're the best man."

"I don't even know where Fort Jerome is."

Lieutenant Robbins opened up his leather pouch and took out a map. "It's here."

Gabe looked at the map. Then he looked at Sally. If the little group in the middle of the desert was going to survive, someone would have to go for help soon. It was probably true that an individual cavalry soldier wouldn't be right for the job, because they were trained to function in units, not alone.

"What about Jack Scoones?" Gabe asked.

"Jack Scoones is dead," Lieutenant Robbins replied.

Gabe spat into the sand. He didn't want to go, but it looked as if he'd have to. There was nobody else who could do it.

"Okay," he said. "I'll go."

Lieutenant Robbins slapped him on the shoulder. "Good man. You might as well get started right now. There's no time to waste. You can take my horse. It's the best one in the troop. I'll have Sergeant Debow fill up a saddlebag full of supplies."

Lieutenant Robbins walked off, leaving Gabe with Sally. She sat on the ground, screwing the top on her canteen. Gabe sat next to her.

"Well," he said, "I guess there's been a change in plans."

"Guess so," she replied. "I wish you didn't have to go."

"I'll be back for you as soon as I can. Keep your head down and don't take any chances."

Lieutenant Robbins returned with his horse, a chestnut with a white blaze on his forehead. The horse was saddled and looked sleek and powerful. It gazed at Gabe curiously.

"Debow will be right here with your supplies," Lieutenant Robbins said.

Gabe wanted to kiss Sally goodbye, but thought it might embarrass her. It would certainly embarrass him. "Take care of yourself," he said to her.

"Be careful," she replied.

Their eyes met, and Gabe felt himself melting. He glanced away from her quickly.

Lieutenant Robbins unfolded his map. "Fort Jerome is about twenty miles northeast of here." He pointed to it on the map. "Report directly to Colonel Sinclair and tell him what happened. He'll know what to do."

Debow approached them carrying saddlebags and two canteens full of water. "Here's the supplies," he said. Debow slung the saddlebags over the rump of the horse and tied the canteens to the pommel.

Lieutenant Robbins turned to Gabe. "Well, there isn't any reason to wait."

"Guess not," Gabe said, pulling his hat more tightly onto his head. "Take care of Miss Barnes for me, will you?"

"I'll do my best."

Gabe turned to Sally. He wanted to kiss her, but felt embarassed in front of all the soldiers. She was embarassed too. They looked into each other's eyes.

"Please be careful," she said.

"I'll do my best."

There was nothing more to say. Gabe climbed onto the horse. It danced a few steps, and then Gabe tapped its flanks with the rowels of his spurs.

The horse leapt forward, with Gabe crouching low in the saddle. Sally and the soldiers watched as Gabe and the horse galloped off into the desert.

Everyone stood silently, hands shielding their eyes, as the horse and rider grew smaller, throwing up a trail of dust behind them.

Sally wondered if she'd ever see Gabe again.

# CHAPTER SIX

Cibicue the medicine man made his way across the hidden valley. He'd been out on the desert praying for the success of the ambush, when a courier told him that Diablito wanted to see him. The courier said that the ambush had not gone well.

No warriors were in sight. They were all in their caves, recuperating from the battle. The women whom Cibicue saw were glum. The heavy odor of defeat hung in the air. Cibicue wondered what had gone wrong. It wasn't like Diablito to make mistakes.

Cibicue climbed the side of the mountain and approached the front of Diablito's cave. "You wanted to see me?" Cibicue said.

"Come in and sit down."

Diablito's voice was deep and sad. He sat in the shadows near the wall of the cave, his leather pouch full of sacred pollen in front of him. Cibicue sat opposite him and crossed his legs.

"What happened?" Cibicue asked.

"The blue coats had strong medicine," Diablito replied. "They rode with a witch who had orange hair, and the witch killed Eagle Claw."

Cibicue felt a chill deep in his bones although the temperature was in the nineties. A witch with orange hair? He'd never heard of such a thing.

"You must make medicine against her," Diablito said. "She has terrible power."

Not far away, Phillip Jones, the captive boy, watched three Apache warriors approach the sacred lake, drop to their knees, and drink. They seemed depressed, as if something bad had happened to them.

Phillip didn't speak Apache and had no idea of what had taken place. He noticed that the Apache warriors carried new Army rifles. All of the warriors who'd returned had them, so Phillip knew that they'd taken them from cavalry soldiers. Evidently they'd been in a big fight. Fewer warriors had returned than had rode out earlier that day. Evidently the battle hadn't gone so well for the Apaches.

Phillip sat in the shade of a cottonwood tree. He felt desolate and alone. His mother was off with the Apache women, gathering food. Several times Apache children had invited him, through sign language, to play with them, but he'd refused. He didn't want anything to do with the people who'd killed his father.

He wished he had a knife so he could sneak up on Diablito and kill him. Phillip held Diablito responsible for the death of his father. But Phillip didn't have a knife. He didn't have anything except his sorrow.

He wished he could do something, but there was nothing he could think of doing. He was only a small boy with no one to help him. He picked up a rock and threw it aimlessly. He hoped the cavalry would come and rescue him and his mother, but was afraid he and his mother would be stuck with the Apaches for the rest of their lives.

Meanwhile, in Diablito's cave, the warrior chief sat in silence with his medicine man. Both were thinking about the military setback they'd suffered. The loss of Eagle Claw and so many warriors was a serious disability. Somehow they had to recover from it and go on.

"Tell me more about the witch with the orange hair," Cibicue said.

"She was as tall as a man," Diablito said, "and fought like a man. When I first saw her, I felt her great power. She killed many warriors with her rifle, and she killed Eagle Claw. She rode at the front of the blue coats, and I think she is their leader. What can you do to counteract her power?"

"I will go off by myself," Cibicue said, "and pray to *Ussen* for guidance."

Gabe didn't want to run the chestnut horse to death, so he pulled back the reins and slowed it down to a walk. The hot afternoon sun burned through Gabe's shirt and hat, and perspiration poured from his body. Gabe was from the north country, and wasn't accustomed to such incredible heat. It made him dizzy and he was afraid he'd pass out.

The horse continued to plod across the desert. Gabe thought of the events of the morning, the sudden bloody ambush and then the unexpected retreat the Apaches had made.

Gabe thought the Apaches could've overwhelmed the soldiers if they'd just kept fighting, but for some reason they pulled back. Something had spooked them, and Gabe wondered what it was.

Gabe had lived with Indians long enough to know how superstitious they were. Indians believed in spirits who could help or kill, and spirits were everywhere. Sometimes Gabe believed in spirits and sometimes he didn't. He was torn between two cultures, two belief systems, two ways of observing reality.

The white man believed in the world of appearances, but Indians believed there was another hidden world that influenced the obvious world. Indians believed there were ways to manipulate the hidden world. They studied these methods and turned for help to their medicine men, who were adept at manipulating the hidden world.

Gabe had lived among white men so long he'd lost his sensitivity to the hidden world. He regretted this greatly, but it couldn't be helped. Sometimes he thought it was a good thing, because now he was less apprehensive about the unknown. He didn't get spooked as easily as when he'd lived among the Lakota Sioux.

He looked ahead at the rolling desert sands. He estimated that he'd ridden about five miles, roughly one-quarter of the way to Fort Jerome. Occasionally he passed phantasmagorical rock formations that seemed to defy gravity. He came to a stream and let the horse drink his fill.

Gabe sat on the ground next to the horse and rolled a cigarette. He lit it with a match and puffed deeply. He knew he couldn't afford to rest long, because the Apaches might mass for another attack against Sally and the cavalry soldiers trapped in the desert.

Gabe climbed on the horse and urged it across the stream. He thought of Sally alone with the cavalry soldiers in the middle of the desert. It was her first time away from her parents, and she was probably ill at ease. He was amazed by how well she was holding up under the strain. Another woman would be hysterical after going through the same ordeal.

Gabe was startled by the sound of a rifle shot nearby. He didn't look around and didn't stop to think about it. Instead, he dug his spurs into the flanks of the chestnut, and the chestnut charged forward, leaping over a stack of chapparal.

Another shot rang out, and Gabe heard the *crack* of the bullet as it passed over his head. He crouched low in the saddle as the chestnut galloped over the desert sand.

Gabe turned around and saw three Apache warriors on horseback twenty yards behind him. They fired their rifles at him, but everybody was moving too frantically for accurate aim.

Gabe hoped the chestnut was as good as Lieutenant Robbins had said it was. The horse was fast, but did it have endurance? Gabe knew he'd find that out soon, and hoped he wouldn't be disappointed.

He rode low in the saddle, his head near the horse's neck. Turning around, he noticed that the Apaches weren't gaining on him. In fact, he seemed to be increasing the distance between them.

"Come on, feller," Gabe murmured to the horse. "Keep up the good work."

Gabe and the Apaches raced across the desert. Gabe continually looked back to check the progress of the Apaches, who continued to yell and shoot at him. It appeared that he was outrunning them, and a smile came to his face.

Then he noticed that the Apaches were stopping. The front legs of their horses went stiff as they slowed down, and then the Apaches jumped to the ground, lay down, and aimed their rifles.

"Oh-oh," said Gabe, as he hunkered down even lower on the horse. He steered it into the dense chapparal, and the horse whinnied as bullets whistled through the air. The horse jumped over the chapparal and plunged past a row of tall saguaro cactus plants.

Gabe wanted to put as much foliage between him and the Apaches as possible, to obscure their aim. He realized that they were probably aiming at the horse, because that was the sure way to stop Gabe. Bullets smacked into cactus plants and shot leaves off trees, as Gabe continued to push the horse through the thick foliage.

They came to an arroyo that was clear in both directions. Gabe turned right and prodded the horse onward. It galloped forward eagerly, and Gabe heard no more bullets.

He'd escaped from the three Apaches, but knew there might be more waiting for him straight ahead. All he could do was keep going and hope for the best.

The chestnut horse galloped along the arroyo, foam flying from his lips, and Gabe looked behind him, not seeing the Apaches anymore. Gabe turned around and faced front again, crouching low in the saddle, hoping he was headed in the general direction of Fort Jerome.

Cibicue sat in his cave and made a doll out of twigs and scraps of cloth. He tied the materials together with string and then affixed the shredded petals of a red flower to the doll's head.

He raised the doll in the air and looked at it. It was about six inches high and was supposed to represent the witch with the orange hair. Then Cibicue lay the doll on the ground in front of him and stared at it intently.

He focused all his energy on the doll as he prayed to the most powerful Apache God for help. "O *Ussen*," he said, "bring your great power to bear upon this evil witch who has caused so much misery to our people. Please smite her and kill her, for we are your children of the desert, and we revere you above all others."

Cibicue gritted his teeth and balled up his fists. His entire body trembled as he fought the power of the witch with the orange hair. He believed that the fate of his people depended upon the destruction of the witch, and only he could summon *Ussen* to destroy her.

Perspiration flowed down his cheeks and chest. He knew that

his people were depending upon him to destroy the witch. The future of his tribe was riding on the quality of his effort. He must make his soul pure and strong. Pushing inwardly, his knuckles went white as his fists tightened, and his teeth chattered. The responsibility for victory had fallen to him. A witch could be fought only by a medicine man. Somehow *Ussen* must give him stronger medicine.

"O *Ussen*," he implored, "please help your people now in our hour of greatest need. The blue coats want to destroy us. We are persecuted wherever we go. Our land is being stolen from us. Please shower your grace upon us now. Hear my humble prayer. Destroy the witch before she kills any more of us."

The doll lay on the floor in front of Cibicue. Cibicue picked up a stone and pounded it, breaking apart the twigs and string, smashing the head, scattering the shredded red petals.

Finally, the doll was strewn in bits and pieces all over the floor of the cave. Cibicue swept up the debris and threw everything into the fire burning in front of him.

The fire flared up, making shadows dance on his face as it consumed the remains of the doll. Cibicue smiled. The witch was being destroyed, he believed. He had absolute faith in the powers that *Ussen* had given him, and in *Ussen* himself. The witch would never bother Apaches again. Her power was being burned up, just like the scraps of stuff that had comprised the doll.

The extended period of concentration was too much for Cibicue. A wave of exhaustion came over him. He lay on his back and closed his eyes, drifting off into slumber.

He dreamed of the witch writhing in pain in a black pit of hell.

Sally was feeling much better. She sat in the shade of a cottonwood tree and ate beef out of a can. Lieutenant Robbins was nearby, also eating tinned beef. Private Milford carried a pot of hot black coffee toward them.

Sally held out her cup, and Private Milford poured coffee into it. Then he poured coffee into Lieutenant Robbins' cup. Sally sipped some coffee, then returned to the can of beef.

She thought of Gabe and wondered how he was doing. She

hoped the Apaches hadn't got him. He was tricky and fast with a gun, but he was only one man and the desert was Apache country.

Lieutenant Robbins turned to her. "Feeling better?" he asked.

"Yes, I am, thank you."

"Glad to hear it. This has been a rough day for you, I guess."

"It's been rough for everybody."

Lieutenant Robbins looked at her and thought she was gorgeous. The sun shone on her clear complexion and made it glow as if she was infused with an inner light. She was graceful, yet strong, and durable, yet feminine. He was intensely curious about her relationship with Gabe Conrad. What were they doing together in the middle of the desert? He knew he should mind his own business, but his curiosity was getting the best of him.

"Wonder where Conrad is right now?" he said.

"I was wondering the same thing," she replied.

"How well do you know him?"

"Not that well, really."

"If you don't know him that well, what were you doing with him?"

Sally looked at Lieutenant Robbins' youthful features, and realized she'd better not tell the truth about her and Gabe. It was so easy for people to misunderstand things. A woman had to look out for her reputation.

"We were going to Tucson together," Sally said at last.

"Was he your boyfriend?"

"No," Sally said, and thought she was telling the truth. She didn't know what Gabe was to her really, but she truly didn't think he was her boyfriend.

"Are you in love with him?" Lieutenant Robbins asked.

Sally smiled, showing her fine white teeth. "What kind of question is that, Lieutenant?"

"Can't help wondering about you two travelling alone in the middle of Apache country. It doesn't make sense."

"We're just friends," Sally said.

"You weren't planning to marry him, were you?"

"No," Sally said, and that was certainly the truth.

"You're quite a woman," Lieutenant Robbins said. "I saw

you fighting the Apaches, and you stood your ground like a man. Another woman would've been crying hysterically.''

"Weren't nothing to cry about," Sally said. "Actually I didn't think much about it. A job had to be done and I did it."

"Yes," Lieutenant Robbins replied, "I know what you mean. It was the same with me. I'd never fought Indians before, but I just did what I had to do."

"You never fought Indians before?" Sally asked, surprised.

"That's right."

"You're new at this."

"I'm afraid I am."

"You mean to say that we're all alone in the middle of the desert, surrounded by Apaches, and you don't know what you're doing?"

"I didn't say I didn't know what I was doing," he told her. "I've studied war at West Point. You've heard of West Point, haven't you?"

"What do you think I am, dumb? Of course I heard of West Point. It's back East, isn't it?"

"Yes, in the state of New York, on the Hudson River. My father's a colonel in Washington. My people have been soldiers since the Revolutionary War. War has been bred into my bones. In a way, this isn't new to me at all."

She looked at his hands, but didn't see a ring on his finger. From what he was saying, it sounded as if he was well-off. And he was kind of good-looking too. She felt comfortable with him because they were nearly the same age. Compared to Lieutenant Robbins, Gabe was an old man. It wasn't difficult for her to relate to Lieutenant Robbins, but there was something remote and mysterious about Gabe. She was half afraid of Gabe, but she wasn't afraid of Lieutenant Robbins.

"Where are your people from?" she asked.

"Boston."

"What's it like in Boston?"

"A helluva lot different from this."

"I guess most everything is different from this."

"Boston's a big city. You don't have to worry about wild Indians burning your house down."

Sally thought of her mother and father in Gleeson. She wondered what they were doing just then, and if they missed her. She realized that she didn't miss them very much.

"I grew up here in Arizona," she said. "It's hard for me to imagine what life would be like without Apaches."

"You might like life without Apaches."

"I think I would like it."

"Maybe someday you might want to see Boston."

"I'm sure it'd be very nice," she said with a smile.

Acting Sergeant Debow approached and saluted. "Sir, I think Private Halsey's gonna die."

"Be right with you, Sergeant."

Debow walked back to where the wounded men were lined up. Lieutenant Robbins placed his tin plate on the ground. "I'll be right back," he said.

Sally watched him walk toward the wounded men. He wasn't as tall or broad-shouldered as Gabe, but he looked awfully nice in his uniform. He also had a sweet boyish quality that Gabe didn't have. There was also something gentle about Lieutenant Robbins, whereas Gabe Conrad was tough as nails.

Sally looked around. The troopers were lying among the hills, holding their rifles ready, waiting for the Apaches to attack again. An atmosphere of danger pervaded the position, because they knew they were outnumbered by the Apaches in the area, and the Apaches now had modern rifles. What if the Apaches attacked?

Sally forked the last of her tinned beef into her mouth. She wondered if Gabe had gotten through to Fort Jerome yet.

Gabe didn't know where the hell he was. He thought he should have reached Fort Jerome, but it wasn't anywhere in sight.

It was late in the afternoon. In a few hours it would be dark. He didn't want to spend the night on the desert. There was only one thing to do. He'd have to climb one of the hills in the area, so he could have a more comprehensive view.

He pulled back on the reins and stopped the horse. Peering out from beneath the brim of his hat, he selected a hill with an easy slope to climb. He should be able to see Fort Jerome from up there, if Fort Jerome was in the vicinity.

He pulled the reins and angled the horse in that direction, prodding it onward. The horse was holding up well but it would have to eat and drink before long. Otherwise it wouldn't be able to outrun any more Apaches.

Gabe didn't want to linger on the desert. He knew that the three Apaches who'd attacked him earlier in the day might still be on his trail, or there might be other Apaches in the vicinity. He didn't want to be delayed any longer than necessary. Sally and the others were stranded in the middle of the desert and needed help.

The horse climbed the side of the hill, and Gabe leaned forward in the saddle. He thought about Sally and realized he was falling in love with her. He knew he shouldn't, but couldn't help himself. He wondered what it was that attracted him to her so. Maybe it was her red hair, or maybe it was her pale blue eyes.

The horse came to the top of the hill, affording Gabe a panoramic view of the countryside, and he saw Fort Jerome immediately. It was nearly straight ahead in a northeasterly direction. His meandering over the desert hadn't taken him too far out of the way.

The buildings on Fort Jerome were laid out in neat solid geometric patterns, unlike towns that grew haphazardly, almost as if the buildings were thrown down by the hand of God. Gabe could make out the details of a large main building with a flag flying before it. That must be the headquarters where Colonel Sinclair was.

Gabe pulled the reins of the horse, to turn it around so he could descend the trail, when something metallic caught his eye in the bushes nearby. Gabe pulled his pistol and swung out of the saddle. He heard the report of a rifle, and a bullet zipped past his ear. Dropping to the ground, he crawled forward swiftly to a rock.

Somebody was out there and had taken a shot at him, and it had to be an Apache. *Of course,* he realized, *it's an ideal spot to keep an eye on Fort Jerome.*

He lay still behind the rock, his pistol ready to fire. The top of the hill was silent. Gabe wondered how many Apaches were out there. Wherever he turned, he ran into Apaches.

He had two choices. He could go after the Apaches, if there were more than one, or he could wait for them to come to him. He turned around and looked at his horse, who was standing still and gazing at him as if trying to make sense out of what was going on.

The Apaches wanted to kill him and steal his guns and horse. Sooner or later, they'd have to make a move, or maybe they'd wait for him to make a move.

Gabe knew he'd have to do something. He couldn't spend all day on the hill, because he had to go to Fort Jerome and tell Colonel Sinclair that Troop C was stranded in the desert.

Gabe placed his cavalry hat on the end of his pistol and held it up in the air. A rifle fired. Gabe lowered his pistol and looked at the hat. It had a hole in it.

Gabe thought only one Apache was out there, because only one had fired. He didn't know that for sure, but it was a good guess. The Apache was waiting for him to move. Somehow Gabe had to draw his fire and make him expose himself. It would be dangerous, but he didn't see where he had any choice.

He got low to the ground and crawled alongside the bushes that ringed the clearing. He knew that the Apache could hear him, and that was exactly what he wanted. Gabe could move silently, but he didn't want to move silently. He wanted the Apache to know where he was, so he could lure him into the open.

He came to another rock and stopped. Then, taking a deep breath, he turned around and crawled back in the direction from which he'd come, only this time he moved silently, like an Indian, gliding over the ground, not ruffling leaves or moving stones.

Finally Gabe reached the previous rock that he'd hidden behind. He paused and took off his hat. If he'd calculated correctly, the Apache thought he was behind the other rock and presumably would be moving in that direction.

Gabe looked at his horse. The animal was grazing on the short tufts of grass in the clearing, not paying any attention to him. Gabe crouched behind the rock and waited.

It was silent on top of the hill. A rivulet of sweat rolled down Gabe's cheek. Then he noticed the trembling of some branches.

He watched those branches and saw movement in the foliage nearby. The Apache was moving across the top of the hill so he could get a clear shot at whoever was behind the other rock.

But Gabe wasn't behind the other rock anymore. The Apache didn't know that yet. Gabe couldn't hear the Apache, but his sharp eyes could detect his path. He was moving to the far side of the rock. Gabe aimed his pistol at the foliage and fired four fast shots.

The Apache screamed and jumped into the air, two bleeding holes in his torso. His mouth was thrown open in a grimace of pain, and he carried his rifle in his right hand. Then he flopped down face first on the bushes.

Gabe crouched silently behind the rock. There might be more Apaches out there. He didn't dare stand up and check out the Apache he'd shot.

On the other hand, there might not be any more Apaches on the hilltop. He might be hiding from nobody at all. Placing his hat on the end of the pistol, he raised it above the top of the rock. No one fired at it, but that didn't mean there were no Apaches out there. They might be wise to his trick. He'd have to try and draw them out, if any were around.

Once again, he crawled noisily on the ground, but no one shot at him. He threw a rock into the bushes, but it drew no response. He raised his hat again, and no one shot at it.

The smart thing to do would be to wait until nightfall and sneak away, but he didn't have time. Sally and the soldiers were counting on him to go for help. He'd have to get moving soon. The only thing to do was make a run for his horse.

Gabe took a deep breath, then leapt up and ran toward his horse. He expected bullets to whistle over his head, but none did. He jumped up over the rump of his horse and landed in the saddle. Prodding the horse with his heels, it broke into a gallop and descended the path down the mountain.

Gabe kept his head low, but no one shot at him. He figured the Apache he killed must've been the only one up there, but he still wasn't taking any chances. His rifle in his left hand and his body hunched over, he sped down the mountain and headed for Fort Jerome.

• • •

"I have destroyed the witch's power," Cibicue said to Diablito. "She can no longer harm us."

They were sitting in Diablito's cave. It was cool and the walls of the cave were moist. Someone long ago had drawn pictures of deer and wolves on the wall of the cave, and the pictures were visible in the dim light.

"You have taken away the witch's medicine?" Diablito asked.

"She is destroyed," Cibicue said.

*Enjuh.*

Diablito looked at Cibicue, who was pale and exhausted from his inner exertion.

"You've done well," Diablito said. "You may go now to rest."

Cibicue arose and left the cave, and Diablito was alone once more. The witch was destroyed, but that didn't mean Diablito's worries were over. In fact, his situation was desperate. Many warriors had been lost in the fight against the blue coats. The Apaches had surprised the blue coats, but the blue coats had fought well, and they'd had the power of a great witch on their side.

Diablito needed more weapons and ammunition, more horses and more supplies. He didn't dare attack Fort Jerome, because Fort Jerome was too strong. He could attack the small ranches and farms in the area, but that would be too time-consuming and the yield would be too small.

Diablito had only one other choice, and that was the town of Gleeson. There would be horses, guns and ammunition there, and the town wasn't heavily defended. His warriors were keeping the town under observation, just as they kept all the white eye settlements and blue coat forts under observation, and his warriors had reported that the blue coats weren't defending Gleeson yet.

Perhaps a quick strike at dawn would produce a quick victory. He'd mobilize all his warriors and completely overwhelm the white eyes in the town. He'd take what he needed and burn the town to the ground. That would pay back the white eyes for the loss of his warriors that morning.

There was a sound at the front of his cave.

"Who is it?" he asked.

"Tona," said a voice.

"What do you want."

Tona stepped into the cave. He was a tall bony Apache, a senior warrior from Eagle Claw's band; he had a fresh cut on his left cheek, earned during the battle that morning.

"We have held a council of warriors," Tona said, "and we have decided that we want you to be our new chief."

"Have a seat."

Tona sat next to Diablito, who lit a cigarito with a match. He inhaled deeply and passed the cigarito to Tona.

"So you want me to be your chief," Diablito said.

"Yes," replied Tona, "because you are a great warrior."

"Are you ready to fight?" Diablito asked.

"Always."

"*Enjuh,*" Diablito said, "because tomorrow morning at dawn we attack the white eyes again."

"Where?"

"Gleeson. For horses and guns. And then we ride to Mexico."

"The blue coats will come after us."

"We will be ready, and this time their witch will not help them."

The bugle sounded retreat and the flag was lowered by troopers at the bottom of the flagpole. Gabe rode past the sentinels at the gate of Fort Jerome and saw the troopers lined up in ranks for the end-of-the-day ceremony known as retreat. The sergeants shouted their daily reports to their officers, who relayed them forward to their commander.

Lieutenant Colonel Horace Sinclair was a short man, with long flowing white mustaches. He returned the salutes and dismissed the men, then did an about face and marched into his office.

His orders were transmitted to the ranks, and the men dispersed all over the parade ground. Gabe rode among them, and some noticed him, but most were on their way to their barracks to prepare for the evening meal.

Gabe had seen many Army posts, and this one wasn't much

different except that its buildings were made of adobe instead of wood. Everything was neat and symmetrical. At the far end of the post, he saw women and children returning to their homes after watching the last formation of the day.

Gabe stopped the horse in front of Colonel Sinclair's office and tied the reins to the hitching rail. He advanced toward the door of the office as the sun set in the western hills. Pushing the door open, he entered the orderly room.

A crusty old sergeant sat behind the desk, and looked up as Gabe approached.

"What can I do for you?" the sergeant asked.

"I have a message for Colonel Sinclair."

"Who the hell are you?"

"My name's Gabe Conrad, and I'm a courier from Troop C."

The sergeant widened his eyes. "Troop C? Where the hell are they?"

"In big trouble."

"What happened?"

"That's what I have to tell Colonel Sinclair."

"You'll tell me first."

"My orders are to report to Colonel Sinclair first."

"Who gave you those orders?"

"Lieutenant Robbins."

"What happened to Captain Donahue."

"He's dead."

The sergeant wrinkled his craggy brow. "Wait a moment." He arose and walked back toward a door, opened it, and entered the next room. After a few moments he returned. "Colonel Sinclair will see you now."

Gabe followed the Sergeant into Colonel Sinclair's office. Sinclair sat behind his desk, sipping a glass of whisky. In front of him were stacks of papers, and behind him was the flag of the United States.

Colonel Sinclair looked Gabe up and down. "I understand you're a courier from Lieutenant Robbins."

"That's right," Gabe said.

"What's your name?"

"Gabe Conrad."

"What were you doing with Troop C?"

"I was on my way to Tucson, and we ran into each other on the desert."

"You're a civilian, then."

"That's right."

"And you say Captain Donahue is dead?"

"That's right."

"I think you'd better tell me what happened. Start at the beginning and don't leave anything out."

Gabe explained how he and Sally had encountered Troop C on the desert, and how they'd been ambushed by Apaches. "About thirty troopers were killed, and six were wounded. The rest have set up a defensive position in the desert, but they're low on ammunition and need help. Somebody had to go for help, and Lieutenant Robbins picked me."

"You're lucky you made it," Colonel Sinclair said. "The desert's crawling with Apaches."

"I know," Gabe replied. "I ran into a few of them on my way here."

"You say Troop C was outnumbered in the ambush?"

"That's right."

"I wonder why the Apaches broke off the battle?"

"I wonder, too."

Colonel Sinclair shook his head in exasperation. "It's hard to figure the devils out. Anyway, we'll have to relieve Troop C as soon as possible." He turned to the sergeant. "Tell Captain Taggart to report to me immediately."

The sergeant performed an about-face and marched out of the office. Colonel Sinclair looked at Gabe. "Have a seat," he said.

Gabe sat on a hard wooden chair. "Mind if I roll a cigarette?"

"Help yourself. Care for some whisky?"

"I don't drink, but thank you anyway, sir."

"Don't drink? There aren't many men out here who can say that."

Gabe rolled a cigarette and lit it with a match. Colonel Sinclair watched his every move, trying to see what he was made of.

"Maybe you'd better see the doctor," Colonel Sinclair said. "Your arm doesn't look so good."

"It's all right now," Gabe replied.

"You say Lieutenant Robbins is in charge out there?"

"That's right."

"How's he holding up?"

"He seems to be doing all right."

"The lad's practically a recruit, fresh out of West Point. Must be hard for him, taking command in a battle situation without any experience."

"He's got some experience now," Gabe said.

"Can you show me on a map where Troop C is?"

"I think so."

Captain Sinclair arose from behind his desk and walked to the map table on the other side of the room. Gabe followed him, towering over the short officer. They stood side by side at the table and Gabe pointed at a spot on the map. "I'd say they're about there."

"Hmm," said Colonel Sinclair. "And they're out in the wide open, you say?"

"They're in some hills, so they've got some protection, but not much."

"The Apaches might attack in the morning, so we've got to reinforce them tonight. I realize it'll be an imposition, but do you think you can lead my soldiers back to Troop C?"

"Yes, I can do it."

"It's going to be hard on you."

"I'll be all right."

"May I confide in you, Mister Conrad?"

"If you want to, Colonel."

"I'm worried about Troop C. Lieutenant Robbins has always been, in my opinion, a rather foolish young man."

"I don't think he's that way anymore."

Colonel Sinclair appeared surprised. "No?"

"He seemed kind of foolish before the fight, but after it he was a new man."

Colonel Sinclair sipped from his glass of whisky. "War sometimes strengthens a man's character. It's the only good thing that ever comes out of war. Maybe that's what happened to Lieutenant Robbins."

There was a knock on the door.

"Come in," said Colonel Sinclair.

A big burly officer with a black mustache entered the office, followed by the sergeant with the beer belly. "You wanted to see me, sir?" the officer said.

"Captain Taggart, meet Mister Gabe Conrad."

Gabe shook hands with Captain Taggart. The Captain had a grip like iron.

"Mister Conrad has come to us from Troop C," Colonel Sinclair said. He explained what happened to Troop C, and described their current predicament. "You can see," Colonel Sinclair continued, "why it's imperative that Troop C be relieved at once. I'd like you to take Troop D and let Mister Conrad guide you back to Troop C. They're right about here."

Colonel Sinclair pointed to the spot previously indicated on the map by Gabe, and Captain Taggart looked at it.

"How soon can you leave?" Colonel Sinclair asked.

"Half an hour."

"Get going. Report back here when you're ready to ride."

Captain Taggart saluted and left the office. Colonel Sinclair turned to Gabe. "Have a seat."

Gabe sat on one of the wooden chairs in front of Colonel Sinclair's desk, and Colonel Sinclair returned to his seat behind the desk. He poured more whisky into his glass.

"Sure you don't want some of this?"

"I'm sure, sir."

"They say you should never trust a man who doesn't drink."

Gabe didn't reply. Colonel Sinclair laughed. "Didn't mean to insult you. I apologize. You said you were out on the desert alone with a woman?"

"That's right."

"Who was she?"

"Her name's Sally Barnes."

"The Sally Barnes from Gleeson?"

"Yes."

Colonel Sinclair narrowed his eyes. "What were you doing with Sally Barnes?"

"I told you we were on our way to Tucson."

Colonel Sinclair appeared confused. "I'm afraid I don't understand. Why was she going to Tucson?"

"I'm afraid you'll have to ask her."

"I'm asking you."

"Well," Gabe said, "I guess she had a little falling out with her parents."

"She was running away from home?"

"Actually I believe they'd thrown her out."

"What for?"

"I guess they'd had a disagreement about something."

"It must've been pretty serious if they threw her out."

"Evidently."

"Did you have anything to do with it?"

"I just happened to be around at the time," Gabe said.

Colonel Sinclair furrowed his brow. "This is very strange. I've known Sally practically since she was a child. She was turning out to be quite a strong-willed young woman."

"She certainly is strong-willed," Gabe agreed.

"Evidently that's why she and her parents had a disagreement."

"Anyway, Sally and I left Gleeson together."

Gabe and Colonel Sinclair continued their conversation. Gabe explained how he and Sally were attacked by Apaches at the water hole, and after a while there was a knock on the door.

"Who is it?" Colonel Sinclair said.

The door opened and Captain Taggart entered, his saber at his side. "Troop D is ready to move out, sir."

"Good work." Colonel Sinclair turned to Gabe. "I guess it's time for you to go. Too bad. The discussion has been most interesting."

"Yes, sir."

Gabe put on his cavalry hat and followed Captain Taggart out of the office. Troop D was mounted in two columns on the parade ground, looking ghostly in the moonlight.

"I've taken the liberty of providing you with a fresh horse," Captain Taggart said.

An orderly was holding the reins to the horse, which was a black gelding with a skitterish manner. Gabe climbed on top of him and Captain Taggart mounted his horse nearby.

"Column of twos, forward hoooo!" Captain Taggart shouted.

Troop D turned to the right and headed toward the gate of Fort Jerome. Gabe rode in front with Captain Taggart and the other officers. Soldiers stood in front of the barracks, solemnly watching them go. Troop D passed through the gate and moved onto the open desert. A wild dog barked somewhere in the distance.

Gabe wondered if Sally and Troop C still were all right. He hoped they wouldn't be too late.

# CHAPTER SEVEN

"I brought you an extra blanket," Lieutenant Robbins said. "It's going to be cold tonight."

"I know," said Sally, lying on the ground near the bottom of a hill. "Thank you very much."

"If you need me for anything, just call."

"I appreciate everything you've done for me."

Lieutenant Robbins touched his finger to the brim of his hat and walked away. Sally watched him go and knew he was going to check his men to make sure they were all in position and ready for attack. Apaches usually didn't attack at night, but who could tell for sure what the bloody savages would do.

Sally shivered underneath the blanket. She felt certain the Apaches would attack first thing in the morning. Where was Gabe? she wondered. Had he got through, or was he buzzard food lying in the middle of the desert?

During Sally's years on the desert, she'd heard of many people becoming victims of Apaches. It'd be no great shock to her if she found out Gabe had been killed. She'd feel bad about it, but it wouldn't knock her out with grief. It was common for white people to be killed by Apaches. Gabe would be extremely vulnerable riding all alone to Fort Jerome.

A woman had to think ahead and take advantage of any opportunities that might arise. She knew that Lieutenant Robbins liked her, but did he like her enough to do anything about it? He evidently came from a prestigious family in the East. What would such a family think if they knew Lieutenant Robbins was going to marry a piece of frontier fluff?

Not that Lieutenant Robbins had actually asked her to marry him. It hadn't got that far yet. But she knew he was attracted to her. He kept staring at her as if she were made of gold. Sally knew she had a small bit of power over him. She'd have to make use of it as best she could.

Meanwhile, Lieutenant Robbins was roaming the perimeter of his position. He saw Private Milford, the cook, lying near the top of a shallow hill, his rifle ready and a supply of cartridges beside him.

"How's it going, Private Milford?"

"Just fine, sir."

"See anything out there?"

"No, sir."

"Keep your eyes peeled. Don't be afraid to shout if you see anything suspicious."

"Yes, sir."

Lieutenant Robbins continued walking. About a third of his men were on guard duty, and the rest were sleeping beside their rifles on the perimeter of the encampment. He'd refused to let the men light fires, so the Apaches wouldn't spot them so easily. He came to Acting Sergeant Debow, who also was on guard duty, holding his rifle in his hands and peering out into the desert. Debow turned as Lieutenant Robbins approached.

"Hello sir," he said.

"Everything okay, Sergeant?"

"So far, so good, sir."

"Keep a sharp lookout. We don't want to be taken by surprise."

"Yes, sir."

Lieutenant Robbins passed him and made his way to the next guard, Pfc. Holmes.

"You awake, Holmes?"

"Yes, sir."

"Make sure you stay that way."

Lieutenant Robbins made the rounds of the encampment,

insuring that his men understood he was in charge and aware of what was going on. That was the best way to instill confidence, or at least that's what they'd taught him at West Point.

Less than a year ago, he'd been a cadet, and the most exciting thing he'd done was go to New York City with the other cadets and get drunk. Now he was an Indian fighter. He'd drawn his first blood earlier that day. If only his friends at West Point could see him now.

He swaggered across the encampment, and knew the importance of showing himself confident and prepared to his men. He could've had a big supper and gone to bed, giving Acting Sergeant Debow the responsibility for the defense, but the men had to know he was actively leading them, sharing their hardships, facing the same dangers they faced. It wasn't good for an officer to distance himself too much from the men, or at least that's what they'd taught him at West Point.

He checked every position on the perimeter of the encampment, and then returned to the spot where Sally was lying down. He looked at her and saw her eyes twinkling in the moonlight.

"Still awake?" he asked.

"Yes," she replied. "I can't sleep."

"Too much excitement today, I guess."

"Much too much."

He sat next to her and took out his pistol, spinning the chambers. Then he jammed the pistol back into his holster. "Well," he said, "I guess Conrad must've got through by now, if he's still alive. He's had enough time. Fort Jerome isn't that far away, you know."

"I hope he made it," Sally said.

"If he didn't, we'll be in big trouble here tomorrow morning."

Sally didn't say anything. She shivered as she thought about shooting Apaches. Could she go through such a horrific experience again? What if one of them shot her first, or caved in her head with a war club?

"I can get you another blanket," Lieutenant Robbins said.

"No, I'm all right," she replied.

"Are you sure?"

"I think so."

"Is there anything I can do?"

"No, thank you."

"This must be awfully difficult for you, since you're a woman and all. I'm sorry you have to be subjected to the danger."

"It's not your fault."

"I wish I could do something."

"You're very kind."

They looked into each other's eyes. Lieutenant Robbins had girlfriends back East, but somehow they all seemed frivolous compared to Sally. He and Sally had fought Apaches practically side by side, and had been comrades in arms. Tomorrow they might have to fight them again. Somehow it all seemed rather romantic.

"You're going to Tucson if we get out of this?" he asked.

"That's right."

He paused and swallowed the lump in his throat. "Could I come see you there?"

At that moment she knew she had him hooked, but she couldn't reel him in too quickly, otherwise she might lose him. "Why would you want to see me in Tucson?" she asked coquettishly.

The lump came up in his throat again, and he had to work harder to swallow it down. "Because I like you."

"I'm sure you must have lots of girlfriends, a handsome cavalry officer like you."

"Not really."

"Why not?"

"I guess I'm not attracted to just anybody."

She paused, wondering what to say next. She couldn't think of anything, so she decided to be silent and see what he might say.

He didn't know what to say, either. His face was red with embarassment and he was glad it was dark so she couldn't see. The silence was killing him. He changed position a few times, wondering what was going on in her mind. He wondered whether she was attracted to him as he was attracted to her. Finally he stoked up his courage and said: "You didn't answer my question. Would you mind if I visited you in Tucson?"

She paused for a few moments, during which he nearly died, and then she said: "I wouldn't mind."

His heart swelled in his breast, and he wanted to jump for joy. Then he remembered Gabe. "What about your travelling companion?"

"What about him?"

"He might not like it, if I come to see you."

"He won't stay in Tucson long," she replied. "He'll be moving on."

"You're not in love with him?"

"I'm not in love with anybody . . . yet," she said.

Gabe was thinking of Sally just then. He was riding beside Captain Taggart at the head of Troop D, and behind them were the cavalry soldiers on their horses, on their way to relieve Troop C, wondering what might be waiting for them out there in the desert.

The soldiers had seen cavalrymen who'd been ambushed by Apaches in the past, and their bodies had been horribly mutilated. They were afraid they'd find their friends that way, and even more afraid they'd be ambushed themselves by a superior number of Apaches.

Stars sparkled in the sky above them, and the half moon sat on the edge of the horizon. A shooting star streaked across the heavens, and Gabe wondered what it meant, because he'd lived among Indians long enough to be superstitious himself.

He thought of Sally and wondered how she was doing. What if the Apaches had wiped out that little detachment she was with? It was a horrible thought, and he grit his teeth to drive it away. He had to believe she still was alive. Otherwise he couldn't go on.

He wished he could be with her. She was on his mind constantly. He realized he was falling in love with her. *What is it about her that attracts me so?* He couldn't figure it out. She was pretty, but not as pretty as some women he'd known. Could it be her youth and innocence? Well, she really wasn't that innocent. What did she have? He didn't know, but whatever it was, it exerted a powerful hold on him.

A cloud passed over the moon, and the desert turned black. Gabe couldn't make out the landmarks, and he wasn't that familiar with the territory anyway. He looked up at the sky and saw thick billows of clouds rolling in. It looked like it might rain. He turned to Captain Taggart.

"I can't see where we're going anymore," he shouted.

Captain Taggart looked at the thickening sky. "We don't want to get lost out here. Maybe we'd better make camp and move out when the sun comes up. The Apaches don't usually attack at night, so Lieutenant Robbins and his group should be safe until daybreak, if they're still alive."

Captain Taggart raised his hand and pulled back on his reins. The cavalry troop thundered to a halt behind him, sending up a huge cloud of dust that drifted forward and enveloped everybody.

"Sergeant Hepner!" Captain Taggart hollared.

Sergeant Hepner, a wiry little man, rode forward on his horse. "Yes, sir?"

"Direct the men to make camp for the night, and post your guards."

Gabe sat in his saddle and looked at the darkening sky. He estimated that they'd travelled approximately one-third of the way to Lieutenant Robbins' lost detachment. He thought of Sally and wondered what she was doing.

He hoped she was still alive.

Sally hadn't realized that the desert was so noisy at night. Insects chirped, birds squawked, and coyotes howled. Cavalry horses neighed on the picket line. Soldiers moved to and from their guard posts.

Sally was bone tired, but somehow couldn't fall asleep. So much had happened during the past few days. Her whole life had been turned upside down.

She wasn't used to sleeping in the open in the middle of Apache country, and felt vulnerable to the elements. What if an Apache snuck up next to her and slit her throat.

She heard something rustle in the bushes nearby, and sat up quickly. It was pitch-black; she couldn't see anything. Was something in there?

"What's wrong?" asked Lieutenant Robbins, lying a few feet away.

"I thought I heard something."

"It's probably just the wind."

"I don't think it's the wind."

"I'll take a look."

Lieutenant Robbins pulled on his boots and got to his feet. He was having trouble sleeping too. The obligations of command were worrying him, and on top of that, the nearness of Sally was arousing his ardor. Somehow he couldn't drop off to sleep.

He drew his service revolver and walked into the bushes, but couldn't see anything. Getting down on his knees, he examined the ground for tracks, but there were no tracks. He returned to Sally.

"Couldn't find anything," he said. "Probably a jackrabbit."

"Are you sure?"

"Yes, I'm sure. Would you like me to get you anything while I'm up?"

"No, thank you."

He sat on the ground and pulled off his boots. "There's something I was meaning to ask you about," he said.

"What is it?" she replied, lying down underneath her blankets.

"I've kind of got the impression that you don't exactly have anybody to take care of you when you get to Tucson. Is that right?"

"I can take care of myself," she said resolutely.

"Doing what?"

"I don't know yet, but I'll find something. I can read and write and do numbers."

"You might have trouble finding a job. Maybe I could help you out."

"What could you do?"

"Help you get a job. The Army does business with civilians in Tucson, you know. Maybe I could convince one of them to give you something."

"That'd be very nice of you, Lieutenant Robbins."

"Call me Frank. Also, I could lend you some money till you get on your feet."

"No, I couldn't accept money from you."

"Why not?"

"It wouldn't be right."

"Sure it would. I can afford it. Don't worry about that part."

"But I hardly know you."

"I think we know each other pretty well, after what we've been through."

She had to agree with him there. They'd been through a lot of shared danger during the past day. "I'll tell you what," she said. "We'll talk about it if we ever get out of this mess we're in."

"It's a deal," he said.

They both lay down and closed their eyes, but neither could sleep. Sally was exhilarated to learn that she could get some financial help from Lieutenant Robbins when she arrived in Tucson. It wouldn't be such an ordeal after all. She was in a desperate situation and had to accept help from wherever it came.

Lieutenant Robbins looked up at the dark sky. The moon and stars were gone, and a faint breeze was blowing. The desert was pitch black and he knew that no relief column could continue in the desert without light. If Gabe had got through to Fort Jerome, the relief column would have to stop until morning.

Lieutenant Robbins hoped the cavalry would reach him before the Apaches. It'd be a helluva morning if Gabe hadn't got through. Apaches were probably out there right now, preparing to attack at dawn. Perhaps that's what Sally had heard—an Apache scout in the bushes.

Lieutenant Robbins rested his head on his saddle and drew his service revolver, holding it in his hand underneath his blanket and watching the bushes nearby.

Diablito and his warriors rode across the desert, the hoofbeats of their horses pounding on sand and rocks. They didn't stop because the desert had grown dark. Darkness was their friend. It concealed them from their enemies.

They could see well enough to know where they were going. They were headed toward Gleeson to get guns and more horses.

Diablito rode in front of the warriors and thought of the legend of *White Painted Woman*.

*White Painted Woman* was created by *Ussen* to be Mother of the Universe, and she had two children, *Killer of Enemies* and *Child of the Water*. One day *Ussen* decided there would have to be two kinds of people in the world. He called together the children of *White Painted Woman* and said: "Here are two weapons. Choose which one you want to live by."

On the ground before them he laid a bow with arrows, and a rifle. *Killer of Enemies* could choose first, because he was older, and he chose the rifle.

*Child of Water* had to take the bow and arrows.

*Killer of Enemies* became the leader of the white eyes, and *Child of Water* became leader of the Apaches. That's how the white eyes wound up with the best weapons.

Diablito wished Killer of Enemies had chosen the bow and arrows. Then the Apaches could've had the rifles, and would've vanquished the white eyes easily. If only the choice had gone the other way. Then the Apaches would never have been hunted like animals on their own land.

Diablito and his men rounded a bend in the mountains. A vast plain stretched out before them. It was pitch black, but Diablito knew the town of Gleeson was down there. He held his hand in the air, and his warriors came to a stop behind him.

Diablito leaned forward in his saddle and narrowed his eyes. Through the darkness, he made out the dim outlines of the buildings in the town. No lights were on, the inhabitants were asleep. Soon they'd be asleep forever.

"Forward silently," Diablito said.

Diablito and his warriors advanced onto the plain. Every man was thinking about guns and ammunition, and fresh horses. They'd strike at dawn, quickly and fiercely, and take what they wanted.

And then they'd be off to Mexico, where the blue coats couldn't follow them.


In the town of Gleeson, Jake Barnes lay in bed beside his wife Martha and stared at the ceiling.

He was awake with a headache and a stomach ache. He'd been sick ever since he'd thrown Sally out of the house. She was his only child and he wished he hadn't lost his temper at her. Now he missed her very much, and she was gone forever. Maybe she was dead. Reports had been received in Gleeson of Apache marauders burning ranches and killing travellers on the desert.

Next to him, Martha lay awake, too. She hadn't been sleeping much lately, either. Like her husband, she missed Sally. She felt confused and miserable.

Jake got out of bed.

"Where are you going?" Martha asked.

"To get a glass of water."

"Get one for me, too."

Jake Barnes pulled on his pants, stuck his feet in his boots, and walked out of the bedroom and down the corridor. He passed the room with the shattered door, where he'd found Sally with the stranger, and stopped, feeling sicker in his stomach.

He wished he'd never got angry on that dreadful night. So what if Sally was being naughty? It wasn't as if it were the end of the world.

Now she was gone. She'd been his little angel, the pride of his life, and she was roaming the countryside with a stranger. Who knew if she was even still alive? He thought of her lying on the desert, ripped open by Apache knives, and he wanted to scream out his anger and frustration.

He continued to the kitchen, where he worked the pump and filled a pitcher with water. Picking up two glasses, he carried them back down the corridor, and when he came to Sally's former room, he walked swiftly past it.

If only she hadn't gone. It seemed as if the light had gone out of his life. And if the Apaches hadn't got her, the stranger probably would use her and abuse her, and abandon her in some frontier town someplace, where she'd become a prostitute, or worse.

*It was my own false pride that did it*, Jake Barnes thought. *If I'd just taken it easy she'd still be here and everything'd be all right.*

He entered the bedroom and passed a glass to Martha, who was sitting up in bed, wearing her nightgown. He poured water into her glass, then his, and they both drank.

"I miss her so much," Martha said.

"So do I," Jake Barnes replied. "I was such a fool."

"I was, too."

They thought of how cheerful the home had been when Sally had been there. She'd been a bright happy girl, and she always did her chores and worked hard.

"I guess," Martha said, "that we didn't realize she'd become a woman."

"We should've got her married off long ago."

Martha sobbed. She placed her glass of water on the night table and buried her face in the pillow. Jake sat on the edge of the bed and touched his hand to her shoulder. "Don't worry—I'll find her," he said. "As soon as the Apaches are back on the reservation, I'll look for her. She wouldn't go too far. I'll ask her to come back, and I'm sure she'll listen to me."

"Maybe she won't," Martha said. "Maybe she'll be mad at us forever."

"I'll apologize. She'll understand. She was always such a good girl."

"I hope she's all right," Martha said.

Jake Barnes patted his wife's shoulder reassuringly. "I'm sure she's all right. She's a smart one. She knows how to take care of herself."


The Apaches left their horses in a gulch with a few of their young warriors, and proceeded on foot toward Gleeson. The desert was pitch black but the Apaches had sharp eyes and threaded their way past the saguaro cactus plants and chapparal.

Their plan was to encircle the town and lay in wait until the first rays of dawn, when they'd attack, kill, plunder and burn. They knew the town was only lightly defended. Diablito's scouts had informed him that the blue coats weren't there.

Diablito advanced swiftly through the foliage, his rifle in his right hand and two bandoliers of ammunition slung crossways over his chest. He was optimistic, because he believed the conquest of Gleeson would be easy. He wouldn't be surprised if not one of his warriors was killed.

He'd visited Gleeson in the past and knew many of the white eyes who lived here. He'd traded horses with them and bought supplies in the general store. They'd treated him like an inferior, although he was a chief of warriors. Those indignities had hurt Diablito, but at the crack of dawn he'd wipe them all out. He'd show no mercy. Death to the white eyes!

Suddenly he heard something move in front of him. He paused, and then was horrified by the sound of a hoot and a swish. His eyes bulged out of his head as an owl flew toward his face and then swerved abruptly away.

Diablito gazed with horror at the beak and wide, round, unblinking eyes of the owl. He saw the creature's outstretched wings and then it was gone, flapping into the night.

Diablito stopped, his breath coming in gasps and his heart pounding in his breast. All Apaches feared owls more than anything else in the world. Owls were the earthly embodiment of the Evil Dead. Bears and snakes had evil power, but none were as evil as the owl.

Apaches believed that good people died and went to the underworld, but bad people became owls. They prowled the earth and made trouble for human beings. Owl sickness was the worst sickness of all, and Diablito believed he now had it. The only way to get rid of it was to find a medicine man who had owl power, but Cibicue was back in the hidden canyon, and he didn't have owl power anyway.

Diablito wiped the sweat from his face. What did the owl want from him? Owls usually told people that they, or somebody close to them, were going to die. *Am I going to die?* Diablito wondered.

Diablito was seriously disturbed. He felt like falling to the ground and passing out, but willed himself to stay awake and keep moving. His warriors were depending upon him. He couldn't let them down.

He took a deep breath and continued on his path toward Gleeson. He wouldn't dare mention seeing the owl to his men, because it would terrify them. They'd want to turn back, and Diablito didn't dare turn back. Without more guns and ammunition they wouldn't have a chance against the blue coats.

In fact, maybe that was the owl's message. Maybe the owl was telling him death was waiting for him and his warriors if they *didn't* raid Gleeson. That realization made Diablito feel hopeful.

He saw the buildings of Gleeson loom up before him out of the darkness. There were no lights and no movement. Everyone was asleep. Diablito kneeled down.

He thought of the witch with the orange hair, and a chill came over him. Then he thought of the owl. Bad medicine was loose on the desert. He and his warriors were facing terrible dangers.

At least they'd have a chance with more guns and ammunition, and more horses. Diablito looked up at the sky. Soon it would be morning. Then everything would be all right.

Diablito heard a sound behind him and turned around. It was Tona, from Eagle Claw's band.

"Did you hear it?" Tona asked.

"Hear what?"

"The owl. I thought I heard an owl in your direction."

Diablito shook his head. "I heard no owl, but something got caught in my throat and I coughed."

"Ah," said Tona. "That must have been what I heard."

"Yes," replied Diablito. "There is nothing to worry about. Go back to your position. Don't say anything about the owl to the other warriors. We don't want to worry them needlessly."

Jamo looked into Diablito's eyes, trying to see if Diablito was lying, but it was dark and hard to perceive anything. Jamo skulked away, disappearing behind a tall saguaro cactus.

Diablito was alone. A terrible quaking came over him, and he dropped to his knees on the ground, hugging himself, trying to bring himself under control.

There was only one way to get rid of owl sickness. He'd have to find a medicine man with owl power to cure him. He'd known such a medicine man years ago in the days before the reservation, but that medicine man had gone to Mexico and was still there, as far as Diablito knew.

The medicine man's name was Niza, and Diablito would have to track him down in Mexico. But first Diablito had to steal guns, ammunition and horses in Gleeson.

"Oh, *Ussen*," he murmured, "please safeguard me just a little while longer, until I get to Mexico."

A wave of warmth came over Diablito, and his shivering stopped. This made him believe that *Ussen* had answered his prayer. He smiled, feeling strong again. He peered through the branches of a tree at Gleeson sleeping peacefully in the valley.

He gripped his rifle in his hands. It would soon be dawn.

# CHAPTER EIGHT

It was morning at the Gethsemene mission in the desert. Father Pablo was in the garden, turning over earth with a shovel, and Brother Leonardo ran toward him, nearly tripping over his long brown robe.

"Father Pablo! Riders are coming!"

Father Pablo stood erect and rammed his shovel into the ground. He was of medium height and wore a short black beard. Looking up, he saw a cloud on the horizon, headed his way. Could it be Apaches?

"Go to the top of the belltower," he said, "and see who it is!"

Brother Leonardo scurried away. He was tall and skinny, with a long nose and a frightened manner. Father Pablo walked out of the garden, wiping his hands on his brown robe. He, Brother Leonardo, and the others were Franciscan monks bringing the word of Christ to the people of the desert. Their mission was just over ten miles from Gleeson.

Brother Pablo was worried, not about himself so much, but for the settlers in the area. He'd heard that the Apaches were on the warpath again, led by Diablito, the worst of the lot. It was very discouraging to Father Pablo. He'd wanted to bring peace and love to the desert, but instead there was war and bloodshed.

He sat on a bench and looked over the mission. It consisted of a few adobe buildings, a garden, a barn, and the church with its steeple. The Apaches could destroy it all in minutes if they wanted to, but evidently they hadn't wanted to yet.

The monks at the mission had been at peace with the Apaches for years. Often Apaches stopped at the well to drink and water their horses. One of the monks was a doctor, and he always treated the illnesses of the Apache children. The well on the mission was one of the traditional Apache water holes, but there'd been no problems so far, as long as the monks let the Apaches use the well whenever they wanted.

But now Diablito was off the reservation, killing and plundering, even attacking the cavalry. Father Pablo knew what Diablito had done during the past few days. Cavalry soldiers, Apaches and settlers all stopped at the mission for water, and kept the monks apprised of the latest news.

Father Pablo saw Brother Leonardo's head appear in the belltower. Brother Leonardo levelled his brass telescope in a southerly direction, and his mouth broke into a smile.

"It's the cavalry!" he shouted.

Father Pablo relaxed. There would be no trouble if it was the cavalry. He arose and walked toward the approaching riders.

They were coming at a gallop, their flags and guidons fluttering in the wind. Father Pablo could hear the pounding of their hooves on the floor of the desert. Clouds blanketed the sky and it looked as though it might rain. The cavalrymen came closer and then finally rode into the courtyard of the mission. Captain Taggart was in front, and he held up his hand. The troop of cavalry stopped behind him.

Father Pablo walked toward them, coughing on the dust they'd stirred up. The soldiers were covered with white powder and wore neckerchiefs over their mouths. Captain Taggart pulled down his neckerchief and smiled.

"We'd like to water our horses," he said.

"Help yourself," Father Pablo said.

"Seen any Apaches?"

"Not yet."

"Consider yourself lucky. The countryside's full of them."

"That's what I hear."

The cavalry soldiers moved toward the well. Gabe was among

them, and he realized that he must've passed close by the mission last night, only he hadn't known it was here.

A soldier pumped water into the trough, and the horses crowded around and drank. The cavalrymen stretched and kicked their legs, waiting for the horses to finish drinking so they could fill their canteens.

Captain Taggart walked toward Gabe, who sat on the ground in the shade of an adobe building, rolling a cigarette. "How far do you think it is to Lieutenant Robbins and his men?"

"I'd say about five miles."

"We should be there within two hours."

A shout went up from the belltower. It was Brother Leonardo in a state of intense agitation. "I see smoke!" he hollered. "Gleeson is on fire!"

Captain Taggart spun around. "Are you sure?"

Brother Leonardo pointed toward the southeast. "Smoke is coming from there, and that's where Gleeson is!"

"Mount up, men!" Captain Taggart yelled. "Prepare to move out!"

"But, sir!" protested Sergeant Hepner. "We haven't finished watering the horses yet!"

"I said mount up, Sergeant! Don't you understand English?"

The men pulled their horses away from the trough, and the horses whinnied angrily. Gabe climbed onto his horse and wheeled it around in the direction Brother Leonardo had indicated. He squinted his eyes, and sure enough, saw a tiny puff of smoke in the distance.

The cavalry troop mounted up and formed a column of twos, the horses dancing nervously in the sand.

Captain Taggart pointed toward Gleeson. "Forward hoooo!" he yelled.

The cavalrymen spurred their horses and rode noisily out of the mission station. Chickens and pigs ran in all directions to get out of their way. Father Pablo watched the soldiers ride away in a clatter of hoofbeats and equipment. They charged into the desert, and minutes later, peace and silence reigned once more in the courtyard of the mission.

Father Pablo heaved a sigh of despair as he crossed the courtyard, covering his mouth and nose with his hand to keep the dust out of his lungs. He entered the cool dark church and kneeled before the statue of Mary.

Pressing the palms of his hands together, he bowed his head and closed his eyes. "Holy Mary, Mother of God, please stop all the bloodshed in this land," he whispered.

In another part of the desert, Diablito and his men were riding hard. Their knives and lances were bloody, and they herded over fifty horses in front of them. In addition they had four wagons full of rifles, ammunition, canned food, and other booty.

They yipped and yelled victoriously, glancing happily at each other. Raising their lances in the air, they thundered across the desert, while behind them the town of Gleeson was an inferno.

Diablito rode in front of his men, a bloody scalp hanging from his belt. Apaches usually didn't take scalps, except on special occasions, and the raid on Gleeson was a special occasion for Diablito.

He'd been afraid that owl sickness would cause him to be killed in Gleeson, but he hadn't even been scratched. He and his warriors had assaulted the town at the crack of dawn, and the white eyes were caught in their beds. The few who'd been on guard got their throats slit before the battle even began.

It hadn't been much of a battle. The men who'd lived in the town weren't warriors. Some of the women had fought harder than the men, but Diablito and his warriors cut them down too. The Apaches couldn't let anything stop them. There was no time to waste.

Now they had everything they needed to go to Mexico. Their efforts had been successful. *Ussen* had smiled on him. Diablito raised his rifle in the air and shouted victoriously. His men echoed his cry, as their horses galloped across the desert.

Diablito saw a rider in the distance coming toward him. He figured it had to be one of his scouts, because no white eye in his right mind would ride toward a band of raiding Apaches.

The rider came closer, and Diablito recognized him as Jasapa, the brother of Jamo. Diablito raised his hand, and his warriors stopped behind him, their horses prancing anxiously on the sand, straining against their reins. The heavily-laden wagons rolled to a halt.

Jasapa galloped toward Diablito and came to a stop. "The small number of blue coats are still alone in the desert where we left them last night!" Jasapa said. "No more blue coats have come to save them. They are low on supplies and ammunition. We can take them now."

Diablito closed one eye and pondered what Jasapa had told him. "How many are there?" he asked.

"About twenty."

Diablito had nearly sixty warriors, and he could roll over the blue coats, stealing more weapons and ammunition, and more horses. He could kill them all, further avenging the years of suffering and pain on the reservation. The blue coats would learn to fear the name of Diablito.

Something in the back of Diablito's mind told him to forget the blue coats, and hurry to Mexico, but something else couldn't ignore such a prize. An easy victory and more weapons were tantalizing to him. He made his fateful decision.

"We attack the blue coats!" he said. "Let's ride!"

He dug his heels into the flanks of his horse, and his horse leapt forward. His warriors screamed at the tops of their lungs and urged their horses on. The Apaches raced across the desert dragging their wagons behind them, heading for the beleagured detachment of cavalry waiting for help in the low hills.

Gleeson was a smoldering ruin when troop D arrived. Everything made of wood was burned, and many adobe walls were caved in.

The main street was littered with the mutilated remains of men and women. Gabe, ordinarily steady as steel, was shaken by what had happened to the town. He'd been here only two days ago, and it was bustling with activity. Now it was an open air cemetery.

The terrible stench of burnt human flesh was in the air. Many citizens had been trapped inside their burning buildings. Some of the men had been tied upside-down to wagon wheels, and fires had been built underneath their heads.

Gabe rode past the general store and thought of how he'd made love to Sally Barnes in there only two nights ago. Now spirals of smoke rose from what was left of the roof. Gabe dismounted and approached the front door of the store. The door was charred and broken loose from its hinges. Gabe entered the store and saw the shelves stripped of most canned goods. The rifles, ammunition, lanterns, and articles of clothing were gone. He walked down the corridor and passed the bedroom where he and Sally had made love. The bed was a pile of junk on the floor. The dresser was chopped up. Farther down the hall was another ruined door. Gabe looked in the room and saw Jack and Martha Barnes sprawled on the floor like bloody life-sized dolls.

He shook his head and returned to the street. The cavalry soldiers had dismounted and were searching buildings for survivors, but hadn't found any. Gabe walked toward Captain Taggart.

"The blood is fresh," Gabe said. "The Apaches who did this can't be far away."

Captain Taggart was deep in thought. He wondered whether to stay and bury the victims of the raid, or go after the Apaches immediately. He decided to go after the Apaches immediately, otherwise there might be more people to bury in other towns and settlements.

"Which way did they go?" Captain Taggart asked.

"I'll take a look."

Gabe climbed onto his horse and rode over the main street of the town. The soldiers had obliterated most of the Apache tracks, but he could spot the marks of unshod hooves in the dirt. At the northern edge of town he saw where the Apaches had congregated before leaving. They had four wagons with them and many horses. They'd ridden off into the desert, moving in a northerly direction.

Gabe rode back to back to Captain Taggart, who sat in his saddle and sipped water from his canteen. Gabe pointed in a northerly direction. "They went that way," he said.

"How long ago?"

"An hour or two. Not more than that."

"Sergeant Hepner!" Captain Taggart called out. "Form up the troop!"

Sergeant Hepner shouted a blistering string of orders, and cavalry soldiers came running from all corners of the town.

They climbed onto their horses and made two ranks in the middle of the street.

Captain Taggart sat on his saddle in front of the soldiers. "We're going after the devils who did this!" he told them. "They're not too far ahead of us! When we find them—show no mercy! Load your rifles and stay alert! We're going to hit them hard, boys! I expect each and every one of you to follow your orders and do your duty! All right now, let's move it out! Forward hoooooo!"

Captain Taggart rode at a gallop to the head of the column and led it out of devastated Gleeson. Gabe rode at his side, looking down at the track the Apaches had left.

Behind them came the cavalry soldiers, rage and frustration in their hearts after what they'd seen in Gleeson. The Apaches hadn't spared women or children. A baby had even been found with his head dashed against a wall. The soldiers hated the Apaches more than ever, and were anxious to fight them. The stench of death was still in their nostrils as they charged across the desert.

Father Pablo watched in horror as the Apaches watered their horses from his well. He saw the wagons loaded with booty and figured they'd come from Gleeson.

Father Pablo could see bloody lances and knives. He even saw the scalp hanging from Diablito's belt. He knew who Diablito was, having seen him on the reservation over the years. They'd even spoken briefly a few times.

But they weren't speaking now. Father Pablo knew his life wasn't worth a nickel. What if the Apaches decided to kill him too? No one was there to stop them. Father Pablo didn't even own a rifle. The Apaches could destroy the mission and that would be the end of it.

Father Pablo and Diablito stared at each other from a distance of fifty feet. Father Pablo was afraid, but not so afraid that he was shivering in his sandals. He didn't want to die, but he believed in the promises of Christ, the resurrection of the dead, the life in the world to come.

Father Pablo even felt strangely sympathetic to the Indians. Their land had been stolen from them and their way of life disrupted. The Spanish conquistadores and Mexican settlers had tried to massacre them from the very beginning. The Apaches were savages, uneducated and wild. They couldn't be expected to behave like civilized gentlemen.

The other monks were in church praying. They'd gone there when they saw the Apaches approaching. Father Pablo had thought it important to let the Apaches see him, so they'd know he wasn't afraid. The monks had always permitted the Apaches to use the well, and the Apaches had never harmed the monks. No matter what else happened on the desert, Father Pablo wanted the mutual trust and respect to remain, if possible.

Father Pablo spoke the Apache language, and he heard Diablito tell his braves to move out. The Indians wheeled their horses away from the well and urged them forward. They yipped and yelled, their horses kicking up dust as they rode out of the mission courtyard.

Father Pablo stepped out of their way as they passed him. Dust billowed up around him but he stood his ground because he wanted them to know he wasn't afraid of them, although his knees were quaking.

None of them looked at him, but he examined them carefully. They'd changed drastically since he'd seen them on the reservation. They'd slouched around on the reservation, and had appeared sickly and demoralized. Now they rode erectly in their saddles, with pride and confidence on their faces. They were warriors again, free of the constraints of the white man's world.

The Apaches rode out of the courtyard and headed north. Father Pablo wondered where they were going, and who their next victims would be.

Sally took a sip of water from her canteen. She didn't dare drink more than that, because it was nearly empty.

She looked around the low hills and saw the soldiers at their posts, sweltering in the sun. The desert shimmered before her eyes, and tall saguaro cactus plants seemed to be dancing.

She removed her hat from her head and wiped her forehead with the back of her arm. It had looked as though it would rain, but then the sun came out and drove the clouds away. The sun rose in the sky, and it was going to be a scorcher.

Lieutenant Robbins was nearby, lying on his stomach, writing his report on a sheet of paper. If he was found dead, he'd want his superior officers to know what had happened to Troop C.

Sally realized with sadness that Gabe probably hadn't got through. He was lying somewhere on the desert and buzzards were feeding on him. She nearly gagged at the thought, but it wouldn't go away.

She didn't think she and the cavalry soldiers would last much longer. If the sun didn't get them, the Apaches would. They were running out of water and the situation was becoming desperate. *Why did I ever leave home?* she asked herself. It would've been humiliating to stay, but at least she'd have water to drink, or at least that's what she thought.

She noticed a group of cavalry soldiers conferring behind one of the low hills on the other side of the position. Debow was among them, and finally he arose and walked across the encampment to where Lieutenant Robbins was writing in his notebook.

"Sir?" Corporal Debow said.

"What is it?"

Debow was nervous, and shuffled his feet around in the sand. "I was just talkin' to some of the men, and we kind of thought that maybe we oughta make a run for it."

Lieutenant Robbins stood up. He wiped his hands on his pants and looked at the men sitting on the other side of the position, who were looking back at him. "Those the men you're talking about?"

"That's them all right."

"Well, let's go over and see what they have to say."

Lieutenant Robbins strolled toward the men. His gait was loose and free, as if he wasn't much worried, and he wasn't. He wasn't afraid of anything anymore.

"I hear you men want to make a run for it," he said to them as he approached.

"That's right," said Pfc. Alden, who'd been in the Army nearly twenty years. "The way I see it, it's our only chance."

The other men in the group nodded. Lieutenant Robbins could see that they were united against him, and probably other men in the encampment agreed with them, but he was in command.

"We'd be sitting ducks for the Apaches," Lieutenant Robbins replied. "At least here we're protected."

"But we're runnin' out uv water," Pfc. Alden whined. "And we're sittin' ducks for the Apaches here, too."

"But at least we're not out in the open," Lieutenant Robbins told him. "I think we'll have to stay here throughout the day, but when it gets dark, we can try to make a run for Fort Jerome."

Alden looked at the others. "I don't know," he said. "Doesn't seem like a good idea to wait."

Lieutenant Robbins answered him. "I don't think it's a good idea to leave this protected position in the daylight. What do the rest of you think?"

"I'm with the lieutenant," Private Milford said. "Tonight would be better."

"Wait till tonight," muttered another old trooper.

"Soon as it gets dark, we'll move out," Lieutenant Robbins said. "That's my decision."

Lieutenant Robbins walked back to where he'd been writing. He thought he'd done the right thing when he listened to the men's idea, but ultimately they had to know that he was in command and giving the orders. An officer couldn't let enlisted men push him around. It was bad for discipline and morale.

He sat down next to Sally.

"What happened?" she asked.

"We'll make a run for it tonight."

"You think we'll make it?"

"We can try."

"Looks like Gabe didn't get through."

"Looks like he didn't."

Sally felt depressed and worn out. The situation appeared hopeless. Looking up at the sky, she saw buzzards circling in the distance. She wondered if they were feeding on Gabe's carcass. Then, almost before she knew what she was doing, she let out a sob. Lieutenant Robbins glanced at her.

"What's wrong?"

"Nothing."

"You were in love with him, weren't you!" he said accusingly.

"I don't know," she replied weakly. "Maybe I was."

"Before you said you were just friends!"

"You wouldn't understand. He helped me when I needed help."

"Did you ever make love to him?"

She looked shocked. "What a question!"

"Well, did you?"

"A gentleman wouldn't ask a lady a question like that. I'm surprised at you. A question like that is an insult. You ought to be ashamed of yourself."

Lieutenant Robbins realized he'd gone too far. Embarrassed, he turned away from her. She looked down at the desert sand and felt forlorn. Gabe had been so strong and vibrant, and now he was dead. She was sure he put up a good fight and died like a man. He was a man through and through.

Lieutenant Robbins glanced at her, and she was so unhappy it showed. A tear rolled down her cheek. Lieutenant Robbins thought he was being ridiculous. They were all probably going to die pretty soon, so why make her unhappy?

He placed his hand on her shoulder. "I'm sorry."

She didn't say anything. The grip of his hand somehow made her feel worse. She was afraid she'd start blubbering. He saw the misery on her face. "Go ahead," he said. "Let it out."

She set her teeth on edge, because she didn't want to let it out. She didn't want to fall apart in front of him. "I'm all right," she replied.

"Are you sure?"

"I'm sure."

"I've got some hardtack in my saddlebag. Want some?"

"All right."

He opened his saddlebag and handed her one of the crackers. She munched on it and remembered the dinner she'd had with Gabe and her parents in Gleeson. It'd been only two days ago, but somehow it seemed like a hundred years.

Troop D rode into the courtyard of the mission. Father Pablo came out of his office to meet them. Captain Taggart, covered with dust and grime, rode toward Father Pablo. "Which way did they go?"

"I'm sorry, Captain, but this mission is neutral."

Captain Taggart glared down at him. "Gleeson has been destroyed, and every man, woman and child in it has been massacred. And you say you're neutral?"

"If we weren't neutral, we would've been massacred long ago."

Captain Taggart wheeled his horse away from Father Pablo. Gabe rode toward Captain Taggart and pointed north. "They went that way!" he shouted.

Captain Taggart raised his arm in the air and then aimed it in the northerly direction. "Forward hooooo!" he hollered.

The cavalry troop roared out of the courtyard and into the open desert. Father Pablo watched them go, then bowed his head to the ground and crossed himself. Just then the bell in the steeple rang. It was time for the noontime prayers. Father Pablo, his head still bowed, made his way toward the church, his heart full of misgiving.

He knew that the cavalry was no more than an hour behind the Apaches. A bloody battle would be taking place soon somewhere out there on the desert. With a heavy heart, Father Pablo entered the church. The other monks already were gathering, sitting in their stalls.

*We pray and pray*, Father Pablo thought, *but the bloodshed continues. When will it ever end?*

# CHAPTER NINE

Diablito sat with his leading warriors in a narrow defile not far from the cavalry position. If he raised his head above the jagged rocks he actually could see blue coats in the distance.

"We will leave our horses here," he told his warriors, "and then we will spread out and surround the blue coats. When I give the signal, we will open fire and advance against them. We outnumber them and pin them down with our guns. We will overwhelm them and kill them all. Then we will take their weapons and go to Mexico."

The warriors grunted and nodded their agreement. It was a simple plan and should work. They'd have to move quickly, strike hard, and get out of there. There was no time to waste.

"Go!" said Diablito.

The warriors left the meeting and returned to the others, where they relayed the plans. Several of the younger warriors stayed with the horses while the rest covered themselves with dirt and twigs. They spread out and crept up on the blue coats stranded in the low hills.

Diablito carried his rifle in his right hand as he crawled forward beneath the chapparal. Through the branches and twigs he could see the heads of the blue coats behind the hills, watching the desert. If Diablito took careful aim with his rifle, he could probably shoot one of them. But it would be better to be closer. He'd have to wait for his warriors to get into position.

He dug his toes into the ground and pushed himself forward. Everything was going well. He looked forward to killing the blue coats in the low hills. He'd show them what it meant to be a warrior.

Acting Sergeant Debow lay on the top of the hill and looked back and forth at the desert ahead of him. It was still and silent, just as it'd been all day.

Debow didn't know it, but the desert was teeming with Apaches who were cleverly concealed and crawling closer every moment. He felt safe and bored. His eyes stung from constant staring at the desert and he was getting double vision. He also had a headache.

He heard footsteps behind him and turned around. It was Lieutenant Robbins approaching, his cavalry hat on the back of his head.

"See anything out there, Sergeant?" Lieutenant Robbins asked.

"Nothing at all, sir."

Robbins sat next to Debow. "Care for a cigarette?"

"Don't mind if I do."

Lieutenant Robbins rolled a cigarette and handed it to Debow, then rolled one for himself. They both lit up.

"I don't think the Apaches are going to bother us here," Lieutenant Robbins said. "Our position is too strong. It'd be too costly for them to attack us."

"I don't know, sir," Debow replied. "I've seen the Apaches do some strange things."

Lieutenant Robbins puffed his cigarette. He thought the men had an exaggerated fear of Apaches. Robbins didn't believe much in the supernatural. He believed that intelligence and courage were the most important factors in war, all other things being equal. He knew the Apaches had courage, but he thought he was more intelligent than any Apache.

He looked out over the top of the hill and saw nothing unusual on the desert. Birds flitted about and the sun was bright and hot as usual. There were no strange sounds or movements. Lieutenant Robbins felt as if he had everything under control. That night they'd break camp and head back to Fort Jerome. It would be wonderful to ride onto the parade ground at the head of his troop, and report to Colonel Sinclair that he'd held his own against the Apaches.

He thought he'd pass the time by making conversation with Corporal Debow. "Where you from, Debow?"

"Ohio."

"What'd you do before you enlisted?"

"Worked on a farm."

"Guess you didn't like it so much."

"Oh, I liked it all right, but I had three brothers and the farm couldn't support all of us. I was the youngest and we all decided that I'd join the Army, so that's what I did."

"Think you did the right thing?"

"Who the hell knows, sir? It's hard to say."

*They don't think much,* Lieutenant Robbins realized. *They just go through life like puppets, letting other people pull their strings. Some people are leaders and some people are followers.* Lieutenant Robbins was glad he was one of the leaders.

Lieutenant Robbins got to his feet. "Keep your eyes open, soldier. We don't want any Apaches sneaking up on us."

"Yes, sir."

Lieutenant Robbins returned to where his saddle was lying on the ground. He sat next to it and took his pencil and paper out of his saddlebag, making more notations. When he made his report at Fort Jerome, he wouldn't want to leave anything out.

Sally lay on the ground a few feet away, fast asleep. She lay on her back with her eyes closed, and Lieutenant Robbins raised his eyes to appraise her figure.

Her breasts swelled beneath her dirty shirt, and he loved the shape of her nose. He wanted to crawl on top of her and make love. Someday, if all went well, he actually would make love with her. He'd get her a room in Tucson and visit her. Then he'd finally feast on that beautiful body.

He returned to his report and wrote that the day had been uneventful so far.

Diablito lay beneath a bush and figured that the time had come to attack. His warriors were all in position. To wait was to look for trouble.

He raised his rifle and lined up the sights of his rifle on the head of the soldier directly in front of him, not more than forty yards away. He chirped like a bird, the signal that the attack was about to begin, and heard the chirping of his warriors, replying that they were ready.

The blue coats went about their business in the low hills, unaware that the Apaches were preparing to attack. Diablito held the head of the blue coat in his sights and squeezed the trigger of his rifle. The trigger gradually moved backwards. In a moment the rifle would fire.

Debow gazed at the desert and didn't see anything suspicious. He heard the chirping of birds, but birds were always chirping out there. It wasn't anything unusual.

He was bored to death, but he was accustomed to boredom. A ten-year veteran of the Cavalry, he'd spent many hours on guard duty and lookout duty. The trick was to keep your mind busy thinking about other things, while continuing to wait and watch.

Debow was thinking about Sally Barnes. She was a luscious young thing and he'd like to get his hands on her, but it looked as though Lieutenant Robbins already had her staked out for himself. The lieutenant always was sniffing around her as if he was a hound dog and she was a bitch in heat.

Debow never got enough of women. Soldiers earned little, and he could only afford a sporting woman once a month if he was lucky. He thought it would be wonderful to be married to somebody like Sally Barnes, and do it with her whenever he felt like it.

He turned his head around and looked back at Sally Barnes. She was still lying on her back, and he wished he could crawl between her legs and put it to her.

It was the last thought he ever had.

Diablito's trigger travelled its final sixteenth of an inch, and his rifle fired. A moment later the bullet struck Acting Sergeant Debow in the back of his head, and his lights went out. Debow rolled down the hill to the bottom and lay still, blood oozing out of his shattered skull.

The other Apaches opened fire, and the soldiers were taken

by surprise. Several of them were killed in the first volley, and the surviving soldiers ducked their heads.

A hail of bullets flew around them. Lieutenant Robbins continued to lie on the ground, and he wrote a final notation as bullets whizzed over his head.

*Apaches attacked in force shortly after one o'clock
in the afternoon. Numerous casualties. Will
try to hold.*

Robbins stuffed his notepad into his shirt pocket and looked toward Sally. She was crawling toward the foot of the nearest hill, cradling her rifle in her arms. Lieutenant Robbins crawled after her and caught up when she was nearly at her destination.

"Keep your head down," he said. "Don't take any chances."

The desert exploded with the sound of gunfire, and Sally's face was pale as snow. She'd been fast asleep when the shooting started, and at first she thought she was having a nightmare about the Apaches attacking again. Then she opened her eyes and realized that the nightmare had become a reality.

Lieutenant Robbins climbed to the top of the hill, where Private Milford, the cook, was stationed. Robbins gazed over the top of the hill and saw the desert swarming with Apaches! They crept forward from all directions, covering each other as they moved. The air was full of bullets, and one struck the sand only a few inches from Robbins' eye.

Lieutenant Robbins ducked beneath the top of the hill. His mind was a blank; he had no idea of what to do. The situation looked hopeless. The troop was terribly outnumbered. He looked around and saw that his men had all taken cover. They were afraid to return the fire because Apaches shot at them the moment they raised their heads to take aim.

Bullets slammed into the ground all around him. He knew the Apaches were drawing closer every moment. Somehow he had to take command of his men and fight the Apaches off.

But what should he do? If his men raised their heads and tried to return the fire, they'd be shot. If they didn't fire back, the Apaches would overrun the position. There was no easy solution. Lieutenant Robbins was struck with the realization that he was going to die.

He decided that if he was going to die, he'd rather die fighting. The time had come for him to take command of his men and make their last stand.

"All right, men!" he shouted. "Hold your ground and return their fire! It's the only way to keep them off us!"

Lieutenant Robbins realized he had to set the example. Clenching his jaw, he raised his head above the top of the hill and lined up the sights of his rifle on an Apache in the bushes below. A bullet whacked into the sand a few inches from his face, and he flinched, but then took aim again. Another bullet flew over his head and a third grazed his cheek, but he squeezed the trigger of his rifle.

It fired and kicked into his shoulder, and the Apache warrior dropped face first onto the ground.

"I got him!" Lieutenant Robbins shouted. "Come on, men! Return their fire."

The soldiers were afraid, but knew they had to do something. The Apaches would be all over them in a few minutes. They raised their heads cautiously and aimed their rifles. Bullets flew all around them, forcing some to lose their courage and duck. The Apache bullets hit some of the other soldiers, and the soldiers collapsed in position. Several soldiers fired their rifles and a few of them hit Apaches, but the Apaches kept coming. The fire was too intense. The soldiers ducked their heads and gnashed their teeth. It looked like they were going to be wiped out.

Lieutenant Robbins lowered his head too. It was suicide to present a target to the Apaches. He realized that the situation was more desperate that he'd realized. There was only one last thing to do.

"They'll be all over us in a few minutes, men!" he bellowed. "Let's show them what American soldiers are made out of!"

The soldiers loaded their rifles and cocked the hammers. Each of them swore to take at least one Apache with him. They all figured they'd come to the end of their roads. They'd joined the Army for a life of adventure, and this was the way it turned out.

Bullets flew around them like angry gnats as they cowered in the shelter of the hills. They knew the Apaches were charging forward and covering each other. It wouldn't be long before the Apaches came over the tops of the hills.

Lieutenant Robbins crawled down to the bottom of the hill where Sally was lying. Her lips were white and pressed together, and she had a wild look in her eyes. Lieutenant Robbins looked into her eyes.

"It looks like this is it," he said.

She nodded.

"I just want you to know that I love you."

"I love you too," she replied.

"Sometimes they take white women alive," he said to her, "and sometimes they don't. If I were you, I'd go down fighting."

"That's what I'm gonna do."

"Your rifle loaded?" he asked.

"It's loaded."

"Save the last bullet for yourself."

He leaned forward, and his lips brushed hers. Then they pulled apart nervously. The Apaches were whooping it up on the other side of the hill, and their rifles sounded like firecrackers going off incessantly.

"I'll stay with you till the end," Lieutenant Robbins said to her. "We'll go down together."

"Don't worry about me," she said.

A few miles away, Troop D was riding hard across the desert, on the trail of the Apaches who'd destroyed Gleeson. Captain Taggart and Gabe were in front, bouncing up and down in their saddles, holding their reins tightly in their hands.

Then they heard the eruption of shooting in the distance, which came as a surprise to them. They tried to figure out who was fighting whom. Then Gabe realized what was going on. That was the direction in which Lieutenant Robbins and his men were deployed. The Apaches were attacking the cavalry detachment!

Gabe eased his horse closer to Captain Taggart. "Sir!" he shouted. "That's where Lieutenant Robbins is!"

Captain Taggart nodded. Now it all made sense to him. He hoped he and his men could reach Troop C before they were wiped off the face of the earth. "Bugler!" he called. "Sound the charge!"

The bugler was riding nearby, the slipstream from the wind bending back the brim of his hat. He raised the bugle to his lips and blew the old familiar call.

The sound reverberated across the desert and electrified the men. They'd heard it a hundred times, but it never failed to rouse them. They dug their heels into the flanks of their horses, and the horses had been in the cavalry long enough to know what was going on. They extended their hooves forward and made the ultimate effort, as foam flew from their lips. They strained against their bridles and the wind, streaking forward, sweat dripping from their flanks.

The soldiers gripped the ribs of their horses with their legs and held on. Troop D raced across the desert sand, heading toward the beleagured soldiers in the low hills. Birds and prairie dogs scattered out of their way. The hooves of the horses pounded on the desert and made the tall saguaro cactus plants tremble.

Gabe was in front, slapping the flanks of his horse with ends of his reins. His horse stretched forward eagerly, galloping over the desert. Gabe was thinking about Sally. Somehow, he had to get there in time.

The bugler continued to blow, nearly busting his teeth on the mouthpiece as his horse bounced up and down. The sharp staccato melody echoed across the desert. The sun shone down on the cavalry soldiers and glittered on their brass and iron as they sped toward the low hills.

The Apaches maintained their steady rate of fire and continued their advance, jumping up, running a few feet, and then dropping down, covering their comrades who advanced in the same manner.

Diablito moved along with them. He was aware that the soldiers weren't even firing back. They were probably too scared. Diablito smiled grimly. The cavalry soldiers had swaggered arrogantly around the reservation, but they weren't so arrogant now. There was nothing like gunfire to show what a man was made of.

Diablito and the Apaches were moving toward the base of the hills where the cavalry soldiers were making their last stand. Their advance was swift and cautious, against no opposition.

Diablito rose to his feet and prepared to dash forward again, when he heard something through the volleys of gunfire. Was he dreaming? Could it be? He strained his ears, and now he was sure. It was the bugle of the blue coats sounding attack.

His step faltered. He hadn't realized that the cavalry was so close. The rifle barrage of his Apache warriors gradually subsided. They'd heard the bugle too.

The cavalry was coming! The situation was suddenly dramatically different. Diablito wondered whether he should retreat or fight it out with the blue coats. His warriors stopped their advance and looked toward him for leadership. Bewildered and dismayed, they stood with their hands hanging down their sides. They hadn't expected this.

Diablito realized he had to make up his mind quickly. Every moment counted. If he retreated, the blue coats would stay on his trail and hunt him down. They weren't so far away. If he stayed and fought, there'd doubtlessly be a bloody battle, but maybe he could win, especially if he overpowered the blue coats in the hills first.

He made up his mind. It was better to die like a warrior than run like a dog. He raised his rifle in the air. "Forward!" he shouted. "Attack!"

Meanwhile, a cheer went up from the parched throats of the soldiers. They'd heard the bugle call too. Help was on the way! All they had to do was hold out until it arrived.

"Hold the damned Apaches off!" Lieutenant Robbins shouted. "You can do it!"

The soldiers climbed to the tops of the hills and leveled their rifles at the Apaches charging toward them. The first volley knocked down a wave of the Apache attackers, but the rest kept coming.

Diablito ran up the side of a hill. A blue coat was aiming his rifle at him, and Diablito shouted a war cry in defiance. Diablito was certain he'd be killed at that instant, and it was a good day to die, but suddenly the blue coat slumped forward. A bullet from the rifle of another Apache had struck him down.

The air was full of bullets as Diablito jumped over the crest of the hill. A blue coat was at the bottom aiming a pistol at him, and he fired. Diablito heard the bullet whistle past his head, then he dived onto the blue coat.

The blue coat was Private Milford, the cook, and he fell on his back beneath Diablito, who wrapped his fingers around his throat. Diablito squeezed hard, and Private Milford's eyes bulged out of his head. He stuck his tongue out and gripped Diablito's wrists, trying to break Diablito's hold, but Diablito was a powerful man. Diablito pushed his thumbs forward and felt something crunch beneath them. Private Milford went limp on the ground.

Diablito jumped up and whipped out his pistol. He fired at a blue coat, missed, and then the blue coat fired at him, and also missed. The two men came together, trying to hammer each other to death with their pistols and fists. Their arms flailed wildly. The cavalry soldier managed to punch Diablito in the mouth, but the punch didn't have much steam in it. Diablito and the soldier grabbed the wrists of each other's pistol hands, so they couldn't get off clear shots at each other anymore. They tried to kick each other in the groin and punch each other in the face. Finally, the soldier lost his balance and fell to the ground. Diablito dropped on top of him.

Diablito and the soldier rolled around in the dust, each trying to achieve an advantage over the other. Diablito saw an opening and jabbed two fingers into the soldier's eyes. The soldier saw the fingers coming and twisted his head out of the way. Diablito and the soldier rolled around the ground a few more times, and then Diablito realized that only his knife could finish the job.

He reached to his belt for his knife, and the soldier desperately grabbed Diablito's face, trying to rip off his nose. Diablito pushed the blade of his knife into the soldier's stomach, and the soldier went "*oof,*" his eyes crossing momentarily in pain. Diablito tore the knife up the soldier's stomach, and the soldier's guts spilled out. Then Diablito slit the soldier's throat and jumped to his feet to see who else he could kill.

Everything was dust and gunsmoke. It was difficult to see what was going on, but he could hear the sounds of men struggling with each other at close quarters. He stepped over a dead Apache warrior lying in the ground and charged through the dust, looking for another blue coat to kill.

Sally was on the other side of the position, lying with her back against the hill, holding her rifle up, ready to shoot any Apache who came near her.

But no Apaches came near her. In the confusion and tumult of the battle, none of them had noticed her yet. She heard the gunfire and clash of men trying to kill each other, and had seen Apaches and soldiers fall to the ground not far away.

The Apaches were busy fighting soldiers. They didn't have time for people who weren't fighting. But then Jamo noticed the figure cowering against the hill. He moved closer for a better look and then her outline became clear to him.

At first he couldn't believe his eyes. It was a white woman with strange orange hair. His response was just like Diablito's when he had first seen her. Jamo thought she was a witch of some kind. He turned and ran away.

Sally was astonished. What had she done that made him take off? It was the strangest thing that ever happened to her. Then another Apache moved within her orbit, and froze at the sight of her. This time Sally was able to get off a shot from her Winchester.

The bullet hit the Apache warrior, and he folded over, dropping to the ground. Sally jacked the lever of her Winchester, as Lieutenant Robbins suddenly appeared through the dust and smoke of the battlefield.

He had a pistol in both hands, and fired them as he walked forward through the swarming Apaches. An Apache with a rifle in his hands ran toward him, and Lieutenant Robbins shot him down. Another Apache, this one with a war club in one hand and a knife in the other, came at him from the side, and Robbins pivoted sharply, firing two shots at the Apache's chest.

The bullets struck at nearly the same moment, and the Apache was thrown backwards by their impact. Robbins cocked the hammers of his pistols, and was beginning to feel that he was invincible. Bullets flew all around him, but somehow he wasn't being hit. Apache warriors attacked him but were somehow unable to reach him.

Three Apache warriors ran toward him, their rifles in their hands. When they saw him, they stopped and tried to aim, but he was faster than they were. He leveled his pistols and fired twice. Two of the Apaches dropped to the ground. Then he cocked both his pistols again quickly and fired another volley. The last Apache couldn't get off his shot in time. One of Lieutenant Robbins' bullets struck him in the throat, and the Apache rolled to the ground.

Robbins cocked his pistols again. He didn't know it, but Jasapa was behind him, aiming his rifle at Robbins' back.

"Watch out!" Sally yelled.

Lieutenant Robbins turned around, and Jasapa fired. Lieutenant Robbins felt a hammer blow on his left shoulder. The bullet spun him around, and another Apache whacked him on the head with his rifle butt as he fell to the ground.

Lieutenant Robbins was out cold, sprawled in the dust. Sally let out a scream and ran toward him. A shot rang out, hitting a cavalry soldier nearby. The cavalry soldier took two more steps, coughed blood, and collided with Sally.

Sally dropped under the weight of the cavalry soldier, and his blood poured over her blouse. She pushed him off her and tried to get up, then realized that she didn't see any more cavalry soldiers standing. There were only Apaches around her. Something told her she'd better lie down and pretend to be dead, otherwise one of the Apaches would kill her.

The Apache warriors nearby didn't notice her, because they were busy taking rifles and ammunition from the dead cavalry soldiers. They'd won their battle. Only a few cavalry soldiers were still standing, but other Apache warriors swarmed over them and cut them down.

Diablito looked over the battlefield, and saw that victory was his. But he had no time to lose. He and his men had to take whatever they could and get out of there, because they could still hear the cavalry bugles in the distance.

"Back to the horses!" he hollered. "Hurry!"

But the Apache warriors didn't hurry. They were busy stealing things. Some wanted the coats of the soldiers for souvenirs. Others wanted their boots. Everybody wanted rifles, pistols, and ammunition. Some searched through the pockets of the dead soldiers, because they wanted coins.

"Back to the horses!" Diablito called again, but no one paid any attention to him. Apaches were disciplined only when they wanted to be, and they weren't in any hurry just then.

Diablito saw Tona pulling off a Cavalry trooper's boots. Diablito ran toward Tona angrily and grabbed him by the hair. "I said go back to the horses!"

"I need boots!"

Diablito was so mad he wanted to shoot Tona, but then something bright caught the corner of his eye. He turned around and saw Sally's hair; she was pretending to be dead only ten yards away. Diablito blinked his eyes in amazement. It was the witch with the orange hair and she was dead, he thought.

Diablito stalked toward her, holding his rifle ready to shoot her if she moved. But she didn't move, and was keeping her breathing shallow. The dead cavalry soldier lay on top of her, unbearably heavy, but she had to lay still and tolerate it.

Diablito approached, and she heard him coming. Terror rose in her throat as she wondered if someone had noticed that she was faking. Diablito stopped and looked down at her. She was covered with blood and he believed she was dead.

"My power was greater than yours!" Diablito said triumphantly.

He felt exultant, because he believed the death of the witch was an omen that the owl sickness had left him. *Ussen* surely had smiled upon him and given him three great victories that day. The first was Gleeson, the second was over the blue coats in the low hills, and the third was the witch with orange hair.

Diablito reached down and touched Sally's hair, and Sally nearly jumped out of her skin. It was all she could do to keep still. She wished she could bite her lip or make a fist, but she couldn't do anything. She couldn't even open her eyes to see what was going on.

Diablito thought her hair was silky and fine; it would make a colorful trophy in his wickiup, representing his victory over the witch with orange hair.

He pulled out his knife, so he could scalp her. She couldn't have been much of a witch, he thought, if she'd let herself get killed, and maybe she wasn't even a witch at all.

Diablito became confused. It was difficult sometimes to figure out who had the magic and who didn't. She looked like a witch, because she had orange hair, but maybe she really wasn't a witch at all. Yet her hair was quite beautiful. He decided to take it anyway.

He grabbed a fistful of her hair, and that was all Sally could handle. She opened her eyes and screamed at the top of her lungs. Diablito was horrified, and jumped backwards. The witch had been dead, and now she'd come back to life!

Sally was completely hysterical. She leaped to her feet and shrieked like a madwoman, balling her fists and jumping up and down. Diablito and the Apaches nearby shrank back from her. Her clothes were covered with blood, her face was blotched with emotion, and she presented a terrifying sight.

Diablito felt terror in his heart. He realized now that he shouldn't have bothered the witch, because he'd brought her back to life! He wished Cibicue was there to tell him what to do. The owl sickness came back to him. He felt weak in his knees.

Then he heard the blast of the cavalry bugle. He turned around and saw a vast number of cavalry soldiers pour over the horizon.

"The blue coats!" somebody yelled.

"To the horses!" Diablito hollered.

He turned away from the witch and ran toward the horses, which were in a defile approximately three hundred yards away. The other warriors retreated from the battlefield and followed him. They spread across the desert in a long wave, but they couldn't move quickly because they were laden with booty. Some wore stolen cavalry boots that didn't fit properly. A few carried armfuls of weapons and ammunition.

Diablito wasn't so weighted down, because he'd taken nothing from the blue coats. But he was terrified. Ordinarily he wouldn't have minded facing the blue coats, because he was a warrior to the core, but he couldn't fight the unknown. And the witch represented the unknown to him. So did the owl sickness. Diablito knew he was in trouble. Something told him he was going to die. It wouldn't be so bad if he could die fighting other warriors, but he didn't want to be killed by the supernatural.

The Apaches were spread all over the desert, running as fast as they could, carrying the spoils of war. They saw the blue coats charging toward them, and gradually it dawned on each of them that they weren't going to make it to their horses in time. They didn't need anyone to tell them what to do. The time had come to fight.

They turned and faced the onrushing cavalry. Throwing their excess baggage to the ground, they loaded their rifles and prepared to open fire. Some dropped to their bellies on the ground, and other perched themselves on one knee. They aimed their rifles at the blue coats who were charging toward them across the desert.

Sally wandered around the low hills in a daze. Everywhere she looked, she saw dead cavalry troopers. The area stank of blood and guts. Many of the soldiers had been stripped of their uniforms. Some had been horribly mutilated.

She saw Debow, and kneeled beside him. He was still, and flies buzzed around the bullet wound in his head. His mouth was open and flies flew inside. Only a short while ago he was alive, and now he was dead.

It was too much for her. She thought she was going to lose her mind. Standing, she looked around. Incredible carnage surrounded her. Only a few days ago, she'd been living a simple peaceful life in a small town, and now she'd been through hell.

She wondered if it was all a nightmare. She pinched herself, so that she'd wake up, but she didn't wake up. She looked down at her clothes, and they were covered with blood. It was hard for her to know whether she was alive or dead. Maybe she was a ghost, floating over the battlefield.

She heard somebody moan nearby. Turning around, she saw a heap of soldiers. The ones on top had been stripped of their uniforms, but the moaning was coming from underneath them.

Sally walked toward them and pulled away the stiffening bodies on top. A familiar form emerged underneath them. It was Lieutenant Robbins lying on his back, his shirt covered with blood.

He moaned again, his eyes half open. "Water," he said.

She was amazed that he was alive. Or maybe he was really dead, too, another ghost of the battlefield.

He turned to her, and his eyes opened wider. It was easier for him to breath now that the weight of the dead soldiers was off him. "Sally," he said again, "please . . . water."

The mention of her name jogged her sensibilities. He was looking into her eyes pleading for help. The Apaches had wounded him, but he was still alive. She had to find him some water.

Getting to her feet, she searched the immediate area and saw a canteen lying on the ground. Picking it up, she shook it and heard water inside. She carried it to Lieutenant Robbins' side, unscrewed the top and brought the canteen to his lips.

His Adam's apple bobbed up and down as he swallowed some water. "Thank you," he whispered. "Are you all right?"

"I think so."

"What happened?"

"Everybody's dead."

Robbins closed his eyes. He felt weak and dizzy, and the pain in his shoulder was ferocious. Everything was so confusing. He remembered the battle and wondered where the Apaches had gone.

Then he heard a fusillade of shots in the distance. He tried to raise his head to see, but didn't have the strength. "What is it?" he whispered.

Sally stood and looked in the direction of the shots. She saw the Apaches hiding behind cactus plants, rocks, and bushes, firing at a large number of cavalry soldiers charging toward them on horseback.

"The cavalry is here," she said weakly, because she wasn't feeling too well herself. She wanted to watch, but didn't have the strength. All she could do was sit on the ground beside Lieutenant Robbins.

His eyes were closed again and he was motionless on the ground. She leaned over him and saw that he was unconscious. He probably hadn't even heard. Flies buzzed around his wound and the corpses all around her. Death was everywhere and it was too much for her. Her brain was overloaded, straining her sanity to its limits.

Her eyes slammed shut and she fainted on top of Lieutenant Robbins.

The men of Troop D dashed across the desert, heading for the Apaches straight ahead. The memory of mutilation and destruction in Gleeson was still in their minds, and they wanted to wreak vengeance against the Apaches.

They held the reins of their horses with one hand and their pistols in the other. The windstream pressed the brims of their hats back as they galloped forward. The bugler continued to sound the attack, and Captain Taggart rode in front of his men, his pistol at the ready.

Gabe was a horselength behind him and a few feet to the right, hugging his horse with his legs, holding his pistol tightly in his hands. He heard the hoofbeats of the troop behind him, and it was a powerful feeling. It felt as if nothing could stop them.

The Apaches opened fire, and bullets whistled through the air. Some bullets hit troopers, and they dropped off their saddles, to be trampled by the horses coming up behind them. Other bullets struck horses, and the beasts snorted as they lost their footing and tumbled to the ground, rolling over their riders, or sometimes their riders were able to leap clear. The ones that did continued to charge on foot.

The Apaches reloaded their rifles and fired again, but the cavalry kept charging, the troopers shouting and their bugler blowing his thrilling melody. Gabe looked ahead and saw Apache warriors firing from behind rocks and bushes. He could see the red paint on their faces and the color of their bandanas.

Then he noticed an Apache straight ahead aiming a rifle at him. Gabe ducked behind the neck of his horse, and the rifle fired. The horse stumbled as the bullet struck him, and Gabe leapt into the air. The horse dropped to the ground head first, broke its neck, did a somersault, and landed on his back, kicking its legs pathetically in the air.

Gabe rolled over on the ground and crashed into a low cactus plant. The needles jabbed into his skin and he grunted in pain, but he didn't drop his pistol.

Horses and riders crashed past him, and dust billowed all around. The cavalrymen on horseback were in the midst of the Apaches now, firing their pistols at close range. Many of the Apaches were trampled to death by the hooves of the onrushing horses.

Captain Taggart found it difficult to aim accurately while on horseback. "Dismount!" he yelled. "Fight them on foot!"

The cavalry soldiers jumped down from their saddles and engaged the Apaches in hand to hand combat. Shots rang out and men cried in pain. The Apaches didn't have time to reload their rifles, and were forced to drop them, using pistols instead to defend themselves.

The battle became a series of independent gun duels amid the rocks and vegetation of the desert, but the troopers greatly outnumbered the Apaches.

Gabe ran forward, pistol in hand, and saw an Apache lean out from behind a saguaro cactus, aiming a pistol at him. Gabe dived to the ground as the Apache's pistol fired, and the bullet zipped over Gabe's head. The Apache ducked behind the cactus, and Gabe shot his own pistol. It bucked in his hand, and the bullet drilled through the pulpy cactus plant and into the Apache's stomach. The Apache hollered and fell to the ground.

Gabe ran forward and fired at the Apache again, to make sure he was dead. Then he jumped over the Apache and landed in front of another Apache, this one aiming a rifle at Gabe.

Gabe thought he was a goner. The Apache pulled his trigger. *Click!* It was a misfire. Gabe fired his pistol, and it wasn't a misfire. The Apache was blown back against a cactus plant, and the needles held him suspended in the air.

Gabe heard footsteps behind him and turned around. Two Apaches were rushing toward him, pistols in their hands. Gabe dropped to his belly as both Apaches fired at the same time.

Their bullets sliced through the air where Gabe had been standing, and Gabe fired two quick shots from ground level, bringing both the Apaches down.

Gabe got to his feet. Turning around, he looked toward the low hills, where he'd left Troop C on the previous evening. Just then, he heard a twig snap to his right. Again he dropped to the ground, a split instant before a bullet fired.

An Apache was lurking in the bushes. He cocked his pistol to fire at Gabe again, but Gabe pulled his trigger first, and the Apache fell forward through the bushes.

Gabe rose to his feet and ran to the low hills, to see what had become of Sally and the others. Suddenly, an Apache emerged from a rock in front of him, and charged with a knife in his right hand.

Gabe was calm as he raised his pistol. He took careful aim, and when the Apache was only a few yards away, pulled the trigger of his pistol.

*Click!* His pistol was empty. The Apache was nearly on top of him. Gabe reached out and grabbed the wrist of the Apache's knife hand, while trying to clobber the Apache over the head with his pistol, but the Apache grabbed the wrist of his pistol hand.

Their chests bumped into each other, as they grappled for any advantage they could get. The Apache's face was only two inches away, covered with red warpaint, grimacing with effort.

The Apache hooked his leg behind Gabe and tried to trip him. While the Indian was standing on one leg, Gabe twisted to the side and knocked him off balance. The Apache fell to the ground, dragging Gabe down with him.

Gabe and the Apache rolled around on the ground. The Apache tried to bite Gabe's nose off, but Gabe drew his head back and the Apache's teeth snapped thin air. Gabe tried to knee the Apache in the groin, but the Apache twisted to the side.

Gabe and the Apache were evenly matched. Both were skilled fighters, with nearly the same amount of strength. They strained and pushed against each other, kicking up dust around them, rolling first to one side and then the other.

Gabe couldn't free his right hand from the Apache's grip, and he didn't dare let go of the Apache's right hand. The Apache wasn't weakening, and he didn't dare weaken either.

Gabe heard footsteps around him. "Shoot the son-of-a-bitch," somebody said.

An expression of terror came into the Apache's eyes. Gabe saw a white hand hold a gun to the Apache's head, and Gabe held the Apache steady. The gun fired.

The Apache bucked once like a wild horse, then went limp on the ground. Gabe was spattered with the Apache's blood. He turned the corpse loose and stood, wiping the blood off his face.

A few desultory shots rang out in the distance. The battle was winding down. The remaining Apaches were fleeing on foot across the desert. The others were lying dead among the cactus and cottonwood trees. Some of the cavalry soldiers were also dead or wounded. A few of them were angrily mutilating Apaches the way the Apaches had mutilated the citizens of Gleeson.

Gabe walked back to where he'd dropped his pistol. He picked it up, loaded it, and held it ready in his hand, in case more Apaches came at him.

"Diablito's dead!" somebody shouted.

A cheer arose from the cavalry soldiers. Gabe walked toward the sound of the voice and saw a crowd of troopers standing in a circle, looking down on the ground.

Diablito lay there, his eyes wide open and staring, his shirt covered with blood.

Captain Taggart approached, a smoking pistol in each hand. "What's going on here?" he asked.

"It's Diablito, sir. He's dead."

Captain Taggart pushed through the soldiers and looked down at Diablito. He dug his shoe into Diablito's ribs to make sure he was dead, and Diablito didn't move. Captain Taggart kneeled down and felt for Diablito's pulse, but there was none.

"This is one son-of-a-bitch we won't have to worry about anymore," Captain Taggart said. "Who shot him?"

"I dunno," one of the soldiers said.

"Anybody know?" Captain Taggart asked.

Nobody said anything. Captain Taggart stood up. Evidently the Apache chief had been hit by one of the wild bullets during the initial cavalry charge.

"Good work, men," Captain Taggart said, jamming one pistol into his holster and the other one into his gunbelt. He turned toward the low hills. "Let's see what's left of Troop C."

# CHAPTER TEN

The cavalry soldiers collected their horses and rode toward the low hills. Gabe was in front with Captain Taggart, peering ahead at seminaked mutilated bodies lying everywhere. His heart sank, because he thought Sally must be dead out there. It didn't look as if anybody survived.

He realized that the girl had been doomed no matter what she did. If she hadn't come with him, the Apaches would've got her in Gleeson. But she had come with him, so the Apaches killed her in the low hills. She didn't have a chance.

It was disconcerting for him to think of such a beautiful woman being cut down by Apaches. He hoped she'd died quickly, without any pain. He imagined the terror and fear she must've felt in her last moments. He was sure she died fighting for her life.

He looked down at the mane of the horse he was riding, and thought of the night he'd made love to her. Who could've guessed it would turn out this way? But the frontier wasn't a garden party. People were killed all the time. The strong survived and the weak went to their graves. Sometimes the strong were killed, too. The violence and killing were random and often made no sense. It would continue until the frontier was tamed, but who knew how long that would take.

"What the hell's that!" Captain Taggart said.

Gabe looked up, and his jaw dropped at what he saw. A person in civilian clothes, with bright red hair, was waving to them from the top of a hill. Gabe's heart leapt in his chest. He'd know that shade of hair anywhere. It was Sally! He couldn't believe his eyes, and blinked to make sure. How could she still be alive?

"It's Sally Barnes!" Gabe hollered, and spurred his horse. The horse galloped forward and Gabe watched Sally become larger in his field of vision. Yes, it was definitely her. Her shirt was covered with blood but *she was alive*!

Gabe's horse brought him to the area where the carnage had taken place. He reined him in, because he didn't want the horse to trample on the bodies of dead soldiers. Jumping down from the saddle, Gabe ran to Sally, who staggered down the hill as if she were drunk.

They met at the bottom of the hill. He grabbed her by the shoulders and looked into her glazed eyes.

"Are you all right?" he asked.

"I don't know," she said in a small voice. "Somebody's got to help Lieutenant Robbins. He's hurt real bad. Some of the other men are still alive too."

She staggered from side to side, and Gabe held her up. Captain Taggart and several other cavalry soldiers ran toward them.

"What happened!" Captain Taggart said to her.

"The Apaches," she replied dreamily. "They were everywhere. Somebody's got to help Lieutenant Robbins."

"Where is he?"

"I'll show you."

Sally staggered over the hill and across the area where the battle had taken place. Cavalry soldiers littered the ground, most of them stripped of their uniforms and many carved up by Apache knives. Some of them moaned, and were attended to by the men from Troop D.

Sally raised her hand and pointed. Lieutenant Robbins lay on the ground ahead of her, his eyes open to slits. A canteen of water was in his hand.

The soldiers rushed toward him. Captain Taggart kneeled

next to him and raised his head. "How're you doing, Lieutenant?"

"Not too well, sir," Lieutenant Robbins replied weakly.

"Where are you hurt?"

"My left shoulder, I think."

Captain Taggart turned around and shouted: "Let's have a medic over here!"

A trooper ran toward them, carrying a haversack full of bandages. He dropped down next to Lieutenant Robbins and examined him quickly. "He's stopped bleeding," the trooper said. "I think we'd better leave him alone until we get him to the doctor at Fort Jerome."

Captain Taggart got to his feet. "Sergeant Hepner!" he hollered.

"Yes, sir!" came a voice at the other end of the clearing.

"Get over here!"

Sergeant Hepner came running on his short legs. His shirt was torn and the lobe of his left ear had been bit off by an Apache in the fight that had just taken place. He stopped in front of Captain Taggart and saluted.

"Sergeant, take a detail of men and cut some wood for travois."

Sergeant Hepner turned around and barked orders. A group of men headed into the desert to cut saplings for the travois. They were similar to stretchers on long poles, which the horses would drag behind them. Indians used them for hauling their supplies across open country.

Other men loaded the dead soldiers head down over the sides of horses, so they could receive decent burials in the Fort Jerome graveyard.

Gabe looked at Sally, who was kneeling beside Lieutenant Robbins, tipping a canteen to his mouth. He wanted to talk with her but she seemed busy with Robbins. Captain Taggart walked toward her.

"I think you'd better let the medic look at you too, young lady. You've got a lot of blood on you."

"It's somebody else's blood," she explained. Then she tore some cloth off her blouse, doused it with water, and wiped Lieutenant Robbins' forehead with it.

Lieutenant Robbins opened his eyes. "Thanks," he said softly.

She touched the cloth to his cheeks. He was unusually hot, and she figured he had a fever. She wasn't feeling too well herself. Raising the canteen to her lips, she took a swig. The battlefield was spinning around her. So much had happened.

She sat back on the ground and stared at Lieutenant Robbins' face, and he looked up at her.

"Well," he said, trying to smile, "looks like we made it."

"We sure did," she replied.

"I want to ask you something. I realize this isn't the best time to ask it, but what the hell? Do you think you'd like to marry me?"

He had a hopeful expression on his face. Sally thought for a few moments and then smiled.

"Yes, I think I'd like to."

"I'm glad you said that. I was afraid you wouldn't. We'll get married by the preacher at Fort Jerome, as soon as I get better, all right?"

"All right."

"You've just made me very happy," he said. "I'm sure we'll have a wonderful life together, if the Apaches don't get us first."

Gabe sat on a hill nearby and watched them murmuring to each other. He couldn't hear what they were saying, and assumed she was just concerned about him because he was a wounded man. Gabe thought he'd take her to Tucson with him as soon as things settled down. They'd get a room together in a local hotel and have some fun. Then they'd figure out their future.

Gabe took out his tobacco and rolled a cigarette. His hands froze in midair and his eyes widened as he watched Sally bend over Lieutenant Robbins and kiss his lips. Gabe nearly dropped his tobacco and cigarette paper. *What the hell is going on over there?*

He rolled the cigarette, lit it up, and got to his feet, sauntering to where Sally and Lieutenant Robbins were. He kneeled down on Robbins' other side, and Robbins turned his head to look at him.

"Hello, Conrad," Lieutenant Robbins said. "Looks like you got through after all. We didn't think you made it."

"I almost didn't," Gabe said.

"I'm a happy man," Lieutenant Robbins told him.

"I'd be happy too, if a beautiful girl had just kissed me."

"That's not the best part."

"Oh, no?" Gabe said. "What *is* the best part."

"Sally and I are getting married."

Gabe raised his eyes and looked at Sally. "That so?"

"Yes," she said simply.

"What d'ya know about that?" Gabe said. "I hope the two of you will be very happy together."

"Thank you," they said in unison.

Gabe knew that three was an odd number. "I think I'll leave you two to make your wedding plans in private," he said.

He rose and walked back to the hill where he'd been sitting. He dropped to the ground and crossed his legs, wondering what had happened. All around him in the desert he heard the sound of axes against wood, as troopers chopped down trees. Other troopers comforted the few remaining wounded men from Troop C, and a detail continued to load dead cavalrymen on horses.

Captain Taggart sat on the far side of the clearing with his officers and sergeants, looking at a map. They were trying to figure out where the Apaches' women and children were. They couldn't be too far away, and they probably had white captives with them. The Apache women would surrender to the cavalry as soon as they realized that their men weren't coming back. Colonel Sinclair would send troopers out to find the women and children as soon as feasible.

Gabe returned his gaze to Sally and Lieutenant Robbins. They were speaking earnestly, and she held one of his hands in both of hers. So they'd fallen in love while he was away. Gabe wondered how it could have happened, but then all the pieces fell into place and it made sense to him. They were two attractive young people and shared calamity had brought them together. There was nothing wrong with it. It was completely understandable.

Now Sally would have someone to take care of her permanently, and Gabe wouldn't have to worry about her anymore. It was just as well, because he'd probably never marry her. He wasn't the marrying kind.

Sally didn't know yet that her parents had been killed, and Gabe decided he didn't want to be the one to tell her. Let somebody else do it. He'd been through enough with her. He figured she'd cry for awhile, but she'd get over it. She hadn't seemed to be that close with her parents in the first place.

Gabe could imagine her future clearly. She and Lieutenant Robbins would get married and become the smart young couple on whatever Army post they happened to be stationed. Everyone would admire them and she'd look splendid on his arm at the local post balls. She'd be a credit to the service and to his career. They'd raise a bunch of tow-headed kids and the boys would grow up to be Army officers, like their Dad, and the girls would be tough and pretty, like their momma. One day Lieutenant Robbins would probably become a General, and no one would ever guess that his wife had lost her virginity to a no-good saddle bum passing through the seedy little town where she'd happened to be living at the time. In time, Sally would forget about Gabe, because he wouldn't fit into the new picture she'd have of herself, or maybe she'd never forget him; it was hard to know what would happen in the mind of a woman.

The soldiers dragged the saplings into the low hills where the wounded were, and lashed the saplings together with rawhide to make the travois. Gabe watched them work as he puffed his cigarette. He looked at Sally talking with Lieutenant Robbins and felt a lump in his throat. Then he shrugged. You had to take what life handed you. It did no good to fight it.

He figured he'd go back to Fort Jerome and buy a horse and supplies. He'd say goodbye to Sally, maybe kiss her cheek lightly, pretending they were just friends. Then he'd shake Lieutenant Robbins' hand and wish him the best of luck. It wouldn't be fun, but he'd have to do it.

As soon as he could, he'd set off alone again across the desert and head for Tucson. The Apache uprising had been put down and he shouldn't have any more trouble. He'd camp for a few nights in a quiet sheltered spot somewhere near water and in time the hurt and disappointment would go away. It might take awhile, but nothing lasted forever.

Then there'd be another town and another desert, and after that maybe he'd go to California. At least he was free, without a woman to tell him where to live and what to do.

He tried to convince himself that he was better off without Sally, as he puffed his cigarette and watched the troopers load Lieutenant Robbins onto a travois. Captain Taggart strode into the center of the clearing.

"All right, men!" he shouted. "Saddle up!"

Gabe snuffed out his cigarette and walked toward the horses. He joined with the mass of other soldiers and found himself a mount, climbing into the saddle. The soldiers formed two ranks, and the wounded men in the travois were at the rear. Behind them were the dead soldiers hanging head-down over their horses.

Gabe took his position at the front of the column beside Captain Taggart.

"How're you doing, Conrad?" Captain Taggart asked.

"All right, sir."

"You look a little peaked."

"So do you."

Captain Taggart laughed. "Hell, who wouldn't be a little peaked in this godforsaken desert." He raised his arm in the air. "Troop—forward hooooo!"

The long column moved off into the desert, and in the distance the sun was halfway to the horizon. Not far from the soldiers, in the cactus and chapparal, sprawled the dead bodies of Diablito and his brave warriors.

High in the sky the buzzards circled and bided their time.